THE BEST
GUARDED HEART

BY
KATRINA CUDMORE

MILLS &
BOON

Published in Great Britain 2016
By Mills & Boon, an imprint of HarperCollins*Publishers*
1 London Bridge Street, London, SE1 9GF

© 2016 Katrina Cudmore

ISBN: 978-0-263-06510-7

A city-loving book addict, peony obsessive **Katrina Cudmore** lives in Cork, Ireland, with her husband, four active children and a very daft dog. A psychology graduate, with a MSc in Human Resources, Katrina spent many years working in multinational companies and can't believe she is lucky enough now to have a job that involves daydreaming about love and handsome men! You can visit Katrina at katrinacudmore.com.

Books by Katrina Cudmore

Mills & Boon Romance

Swept into the Rich Man's World

Visit the Author Profile page at millsandboon.co.uk.

To Fin, your unwavering support and love
has made this book possible.
You are my life.

CHAPTER ONE

SOFIA'S VOICEMAIL. AGAIN. Grace Chapman gave her smartphone's contact photo of her best friend a death stare and muttered, 'You can hide, Sofia, but I'll find you.'

Grace loved Sofia to bits; during the madness of the past few years she'd been her rock of cheerful good sense. But every now and again, when life got too intense, Sofia lost the plot big-time. Like today. Yes, Grace might have missed her flight and ended up arriving in Athens seven hours late. But she'd had everything under control. Until Sofia had obviously panicked and called in the big guns: the Petrakis family. Which meant that instead of catching the last ferry of the day at Piraeus port, as she had hoped, Grace was now stuck in the VIP lounge of Athens airport, awaiting the arrival of Sofia's soon-to-be father-in-law. A man who brought the word *intimidating* to a whole new level of meaning.

Sofia would have thought she was helping; but in truth she had totally messed up Grace's already tight schedule. There was no way, now, that she would make it to Sofia's wedding venue, Kasas Island, in time for the flower delivery in the morning.

She wasn't going to panic.

Okay, she *was* panicking.

Less than three days to prepare and organise the flowers for the Greek society wedding of the year.

Three days that would determine the success or failure of her dream to establish her name as a leading wedding floral designer. Three days to prove that she wasn't *'a clueless dreamer'*.

This morning, full of enthusiasm, she had thought she could take on the world. Now she just felt embarrassed and out of her depth.

She pushed the untouched champagne flute the lounge hostess had presented to her further away. Her stomach felt as though it was off doing a moon walk without her.

The lounge door swept open. And her stomach headed into orbit at the prospect of being at the receiving end of Mr Petrakis's surly manner.

But standing at the far end of the airport lounge was *not* the older man she had expected. Instead, penetrating eyes scanned the room and came to a land on her. Long tanned fingers shot upwards. His eyes continued to bore into hers. With a quick tug, he unravelled his bow tie, leaving it to hang lose.

Her smile wavered. She took in the chiselled bone structure, the confidence of his stride as he walked towards her, the perfection of his tuxedo. The tousled disarray of his dark brown hair that made him look as though he had just climbed out of bed.

'Miss Chapman?'

His voice was smooth and refined. If Central Casting was ever looking for a new Bond he would be a shoo-in. Her already racing heart galloped even faster.

Her seat was low and he seemed impossibly tall and menacing as he stood over her.

Clumsily she clambered out of it and tugged down on the hem of her yellow sundress, which suddenly felt too short and casual in the presence of his designer tux and expensive cologne. She was a low-budget package tourist to his first-class sophistication.

His eyes ran leisurely over the length of her body. Her insides melted. A thick dark eyebrow rose as he waited for her to speak, but for the first time in her life no meaningful words jangled in her brain. Instead it was a wasteland of inappropriate thoughts of lust for the man who stood before her.

Just above his left eyebrow a sickle-shaped scar became more prominent as his frown deepened. She balled her hands, worried that she'd give in to temptation and reach out and run her thumb against it.

After another excruciating few seconds of silence she eventually managed to garble out, 'Yes... Yes, I'm Grace Chapman. I was expecting Mr Petrakis. The airport ground staff told me he had asked that I stay here until he arrived.'

With a quick nod he answered, 'Yes I did.'

'Oh.' It slowly dawned on her who he was. '*Oh!* You must be Andreas... Christos's brother. I thought it was your father who had sent the message. He and I met in London last month, at Christos and Sofia's engagement party.' Grace held out her hand. 'You're the best man, I believe?'

He paused for a second before smooth warm skin enclosed her hand. His handshake was firm, the dominant clasp of a powerful man who liked to get his own way.

In her flat sandals she had to arch her neck to meet his stare. Piercing green eyes framed by long dark eyelashes studied her, and his head was thrown back at an arrogant tilt. The apple really hadn't fallen far from the tree. Dark stubble lined smooth golden skin.

'And I believe *you're* to be the chief bridesmaid?'

She ignored the coolness of his tone and let her enthusiasm for the upcoming wedding take over. 'Yes—and also the wedding floral designer. Sofia and I have been best friends for years. It's a shame you missed the engagement party—we had such fun.'

He gave an indifferent shrug and then his mouth curled derisively. 'You missed your flight.'

Her heart leapt at his reproachful tone. About to explain why, she stopped. He really didn't look as if he was in the mood to hear about delayed trains. Instead she said, 'Yes, unfortunately. Now my priority is to get to Kasas as soon as possible.'

'You've missed the last ferry.'

She forced herself not to say something terse and gave a polite smile. 'Yes, I know.' Her smile wobbled. *Don't say anything. Remain calm. I'm sure he doesn't mean to be so arrogant.* Her good intentions lasted all of one second. 'My flight did arrive in time for me to catch the ferry. I had a taxi waiting.'

His mouth thinned. 'And tomorrow the sun will rise in the west…'

Well, really! Frustration hummed in her ears. 'I had an hour.'

He scowled at her, making no effort to conceal his growing irritation. 'Christos realised you would miss the ferry so he called me and asked that I collect you.'

Her frustration gave way to embarrassment. His superior attitude might be rubbing her up the wrong way, but she had to face the fact that his night had obviously ended abruptly because of her.

She gestured to his tux and said, 'I hope I didn't disturb your night out.'

Something flashed in the depths of his eyes. Was it annoyance or some other memory? Had he been with someone? Sofia had said he had a reputation for being a playboy. Maybe she had been right about that tousled hair. It was still relatively early...but then what did *she* know about the bedroom habits of playboys? None of her exes had ever come close to being as dangerously lethal as the man standing before her.

'No doubt Sofia panicked and got Christos to call you. She's worried I'll get lost. It's my first time in Greece. In fact it's my first time being abroad on my own.'

Those dark eyebrows narrowed. He studied her incredulously. An awkward silence followed.

She said the first thing that came into her head. 'I suppose you spend your days travelling...what with your business and everything?'

He tilted his head and gazed at her suspiciously. 'Have you been doing your homework on me?'

'No!' Her cheeks grew hot and she cringed to think he might assume she was blushing out of guilt. 'Of course not. I only know what Sofia told me...that you are Christos's older brother.'

The eldest son of the wealthy and powerful Petrakis family, in fact, who had gone on to amass his own fortune in construction and property.

As he continued to gaze at her sceptically she added, 'I've only met Christos a few times, but from the moment I met him I knew that he and Sofia were perfect for one another. I'm so happy for Sofia. And her dad is equally thrilled that she's marrying a fellow Greek.'

Uncomfortable at the way he studied her, and trying to ignore just how gauche she felt in front of this much too silent and urbane man, she decided to change the subject to something that puzzled her. She gestured towards the other waiting travellers, and frowned when she saw that the other two women in the room, both much more elegantly groomed for the VIP lounge than she was, were staring at Andreas with obvious appreciation.

'How did you know who I was?'

He reached into the inner pocket of his jacket and took out a phone. After a few quick swipes he handed it to her. A photo of her and Sofia pulling silly faces at the camera popped up on the screen. Christos had taken the photo last weekend, after Sofia's hen party in London…they'd both had one too many mojitos. Grace gave a squeal of despair.

For the briefest of moments a faint hint of amusement lifted his mouth upwards, but it faded and he said with a note of exasperation, 'Christos is flooding my email with photos of Sofia.'

Confused by his tone, she decided to ignore it and handed Andreas back his phone. 'That's so cute. They're so in love. Sofia tells me that Kasas is incredibly romantic. She truly appreciates you hosting the wedding there.'

He deposited the phone back in his pocket and folded his arms. The side of his upper lip curled upwards. Lord, he had a beautiful mouth. Wide, with lips that were much too full. A mouth that promised endless sleepless nights.

She gave herself a mental shake. She had enough on her plate with the wedding flowers. Getting distracted by this Greek god standing in front of her was definitely not a good idea.

He gestured to her chair. 'Please—take a seat. I think we should discuss your stay on Kasas.'

Puzzled, she sat back down and wished once again that she had worn a longer dress as her hem rode up the length of her legs. When she glanced up, Andreas was sitting opposite her, his eyes trained on her bare legs. When their eyes met she saw a hint of appreciation. But then he inhaled a deep breath and moved forward to lean his elbows on his thighs, the wool of his trousers stretching over hard muscle.

'I had intended taking you to Kasas tonight—'

She could not help but interrupt as relief flooded her veins. 'That would be *fantastic*. The flowers and all the other supplies are being delivered early tomorrow morning, and I need to be there to—'

His hand slashed down through the air to halt her interruption with his own. 'Yes, but considering that you've never been to Greece before why don't I arrange for the wedding planner to organise the flowers? You can spend the next few days travelling. Kasas is isolated. It would be much more enjoyable for you to explore Greece instead. As I'm returning to the island for the rest of the week, you are welcome to use my apartment and the services of my chauffeur here in Athens.'

Her mouth dropped open. Was he being serious?

'But I'm the florist for the wedding.' Through her confusion a horrible thought occurred. 'Christos *did* tell you that I would be arriving early to create all the floral arrangements, didn't he? This has been planned for weeks.'

'He may have mentioned it…amongst all the chaos of the other wedding plans. I hadn't appreciated that you would be staying for so long.'

Heat flared even more brightly on her cheeks. He clearly wasn't keen on her staying on the island. And he obviously had no idea or appreciation for the work and skill involved in flower design.

Memories of her father's sneering comments about her making a living by *'playing with flowers'* had her saying in the politest voice she could muster, 'I appreciate your offer, but tomorrow morning I have over a thousand flowers being delivered to the island. It's essential that I'm there to coordinate their arrival. I take my job very seriously, Mr Petrakis. That's why I've spent the past month planning the designs, sourcing the flowers and organising support florists from nearby islands. I'm not going to walk away from my commitments now to go on *holiday*.'

His jaw tightened and he fixed her with an intense stare. 'My island is secluded. There is only my villa. No shops or bars to entertain you.'

She could not help but give a light laugh. 'I'm not here for shopping or the nightlife.'

'I'm concerned that you will be bored in the evenings, when the wedding planner and her team have left the island. Apart from my married housekeeper and a gardener, who live in a separate villa, there will be no other people around.'

His eyes, filled with a masculine heat, held hers and a surge of tense energy passed between them.

He came a little closer and in a low growl added, 'It will only be you and me.'

For a crazy moment something primal, something beyond comprehension, crackled in the air between them. Heat flared in every cell of her body. Her breath caught as a wave of longing…of desire…rippled through her.

His eyes grew darker as he held her stare, and a slash of heat appeared on his cheeks.

He looked away abruptly, his jaw tightening as he cleared his throat. 'I'll be working late each evening, so I won't be available to entertain you.'

Grace blinked. And blinked again. She felt dizzy with the desire to move towards him, to inhabit his space, to inhale his scent, to feel the heat of his body. What was happening to her?

For the past month she had been so excited about this trip—at the prospect of finally establishing her name as a florist, of finding her freedom. And now her bubble of happiness had truly burst.

Should she take up his offer? The prospect of spending nights alone with him in the seclusion of his island with virtually no one else around was daunting. A strange tug of war of deep attraction and irritation was raging between them…and she wanted to run away from it. And, after years of dealing with her father's unforgiving attitude, did she honestly want to spend time with a man who would be happier if she wasn't there?

But this wedding was about celebrating Sofia and Christos's love. She wasn't going to let Andreas Petrakis stand in the way of her making sure they had the perfect flowers to represent that love and commitment. There was no way he was stopping her from creating Sofia's bouquet—which she intended to do by weaving all her love for her best friend into the design. And she had to remember the importance of this wedding in establishing her career.

So she gave him a brief smile and tried to inject a brusque, no-argument tone to her voice. 'Thank you, but I'm perfectly fine with my own company. I'm here to ensure that the flowers are spectacular on the wedding day, so I'll be extremely busy and certainly won't get in your way. And please don't worry about me missing out. I plan on touring Greece once the wedding is over.'

With that she stood, lifted her weekend bag up and grabbed her heavy pull-along suitcase.

'Now, if it's okay with you, I would like to leave.'

Grace was standing at the edge of the clifftop path that led from the helipad down to Andreas's villa, her weekend bag at her feet. As he neared her the helicopter lifted off to return to Athens, and her hands rushed down to capture the billowing material of her dress as it rose up to expose even more inches of her legs—legs that he had spent the past hour trying not to stare at.

They weren't the longest legs he had ever seen, but there was something about those toned but full thighs and cute dimpled knees that had him fantasising about her in incredibly inappropriate ways. Even as he had stared out into the night sky as they had been flown here images of his fingers trailing along the smooth creamy skin of her thighs had plagued him.

They had barely spoken on the journey, and her quietness surprised him. At the airport she had seemed such an overexcited chatterbox. Had his welcome been too brusque? After all, it wasn't *her* fault that earlier that night at a charity gala ball in the Hotel Grande Bretagne he had been only too aware of the other guests' deliberate avoidance of discussing Christos's upcoming wedding with him. And then Christos had rung to explain that the chief bridesmaid had missed her flight. Asked would he mind rescuing her.

Why on earth had he agreed to host the wedding in the first place? It was getting more complicated by the day...and bringing back humiliating memories he had spent the past two years burying.

Yes, he had vaguely agreed to Grace Chapman's early arrival, but he hadn't expected her to be so elated about the wedding or so distractingly beautiful. Her excitement had brought home just how much he hated the prospect of this wedding. And, unbelievably, this was her first time abroad on her own. He didn't have time to babysit her—not with the serious issues complicating the construction of his new resort on the Cayman Islands. He urgently needed to resolve them to stop further haemorrhaging of the project's finances. Having her on the island was a headache he didn't need right now.

Unfortunately she had other ideas.

'This view is absolutely stunning.'

She didn't turn to him when she spoke, but continued to gaze towards the lights of Naxos in the distance. The sky was a never-ending celestial ocean of stars. Beneath them, far below the cliff-face, the Aegean Sea crashed onto the shore.

She gave a light shiver and rubbed her hands against her bare arms. A silver bracelet jangled at her wrist. He instinctively shrugged off his jacket. When he held it out for her to put on she jerked back in surprise. In the darkness he could just about see the violet-blue depths of her eyes. Eyes that had swallowed his soul for a foolish few seconds at the airport.

Initially she looked as though she would refuse his offer, but then she gave a nod of acceptance. She turned around and pushed her arms into the sleeves. When he pulled it up to her slim shoulders she moved at the same time to sweep up the long length of her golden blonde hair trapped beneath the jacket. Her hair fell against his hands like the gentle weight of silk, her floral scent carried with it. His gut tightened. And when she turned those huge eyes to him they were full of questions, of awareness of the chemistry sizzling between them. He itched to touch the smooth line of her jaw, to run his thumb over the sensual plumpness of her lips.

He took a step away.

She twisted back towards the sea, her shoulders sagging faintly before she went to pick up her weekend bag, but he whipped it up, along with her suitcase.

'The path down to the villa is well lit, but still be careful—it's steep. *Ela.* Come. I will lead the way.'

On the way down the path he paused a number of times, to allow her to catch up and to ensure that she was following him safely. As they rounded the corner that opened up the villa to their view he heard her gasp. He turned in alarm. Grace stood staring at the villa, its walls bathed in the light from the terraces.

'What a stunning building—it's like a stack of sugar cubes perched on the mountainside! How absolutely beautiful.'

Memories of the last woman he had brought here stirred at her words. He pushed them away. 'Thank you. I'll show you to your room as it's getting late. In the morning you can look around the villa and the gardens.'

Instead of following him Grace moved to the furthest reaches of one of the terraces and leaned on the balustrade.

'Now I understand why Christos was so eager to marry here. It's an idyllic wedding location. Sofia showed me some photos, but I had no idea it was so lovely. I can just imagine how incredible it will look on the night of the wedding, when everyone is dancing out here on the terrace, candles lit...'

It was time to move her on. 'As I said, I'll show you to your bedroom and then you can join me for something to eat.'

She stepped more fully into the light of the terrace, as though she didn't want to speak from the shadows. His jacket hung loose on her, almost reaching down to the hem of her dress.

'Thanks, but I'm not hungry.' She wrapped the jacket around her body, folding her arms over it to secure it closed. 'You're not excited about the wedding?'

He paused as he calculated his best response. Time to put his cards on the table. 'I'm concerned that they are rushing into this. They barely know one another. How long have they been together? Four months? The whole thing is unwise.'

'But they are really happy. I've never seen a couple so in love...so right for one another. It truly was love at first sight for them both.'

The gentle wistfulness in her voice had him clenching his fists.

'Really? Love at first sight?'

'Yes—why not?'

Her idealism made him want to be cruel, to shake her out of her romantic bubble. '*Lust* at first sight, maybe.'

Silence followed his words and they stared at each other, the truth of his words, as applied to them, hanging in the space between them.

He forced himself to continue. 'It takes a long time to get to know another person—if you ever can. People aren't what they seem.'

'I'm not sure what you mean.'

'My brother is an exceptionally wealthy man.'

She studied him with a mixed expression of disappointment and hurt. 'That means nothing to Sofia, trust me.'

For a brief moment he hated himself for his cynicism, for causing that wounded expression. But then he remembered how he had been played for a fool before, and he asked with a bitter laugh, 'Do you seriously believe that?'

Hard resolution entered her eyes. 'Yes. Absolutely.' She walked back to him, anger clear in her quick pace, in the way she glared at him.

Well, tough. He would remain convinced that Sofia was marrying Christos for his name and wealth until it was proved otherwise. And as for Grace Chapman... She seemed to know a lot about him. Was she really here just

to organise the wedding flowers? Or did she perhaps hope
for romance with the best man?

And that wasn't his vanity speaking. He had a constant
stream of women eager to date him—to date a Petrakis,
date a billionaire. To date him for all the superficial reasons he hated. But it suited him, because no woman was
ever getting close to knowing the real him again. And
no way was he getting entangled with the chief bridesmaid when tradition dictated that they would see each
other in the future.

He picked up her suitcase and said once again, 'I'll
show you to your room.'

Her phone rang. She checked the screen and turned
away. 'Hi, Matt.' A long giggle followed. 'Of *course* I
miss you.'

As he took her bags up into the villa he gritted his
teeth at how happy she sounded. When was the last time
someone had answered *his* call with such warmth and
tenderness? And then anger surged through his veins.
Was she already in a relationship? If so, why the hell was
she allowing the chemistry between them to smoulder on?

'I love you too.'

Grace hung up from Matt and stretched her neck back,
easing the tension in her muscles a fraction.

She rolled her shoulders and took in once again the
quiet serenity of her surroundings. Then she steeled herself. She walked into the villa and entered a large living
room, seeing walls whitewashed in gentle curves, a re-
cessed fireplace. The stillness of the room and its simple
refined beauty, from the huge white sofas on white marble floors to the handcrafted teak furniture, were at odds
with the sense of injustice raging in her heart.

Andreas had no right to make such horrible assumptions about Sofia. She closed her eyes and inhaled deeply. Was Andreas just like her father? Cold and cynical? A man so obsessed with becoming wealthy he was blind to the magic of love and loyalty?

Whatever the truth, Sofia and Christos could not arrive to find the best man and chief bridesmaid at loggerheads. She and Andreas would have to learn to get on.

She found him in the kitchen, propped against the countertop, peeling an orange. She placed his jacket on the back of a chair. Unconsciously, she let her hand linger for a few moments on the soft wool, until she realised what she was doing.

Long elegant fingers expertly spiralled the peel off the orange, but he didn't glance downwards once to watch his progress—instead he studied her.

She placed a bottle of champagne on the counter. In response to his frown she explained, 'It's a thank-you for having me to stay.'

She had thought it might be an appropriate gift, given the upcoming celebrations, but was rapidly revising *that* idea. She twisted the bracelet at her wrist, her fingers reaching for the two charms that sat at its centre. The tension in her body eased a fraction when she squeezed the silver metal with her thumb and forefinger.

'I think we need to talk.'

He gave a tight nod and walked over to a cupboard. He opened the door on an array of crystal glasses. 'What can I get you to drink? Wine? Beer?'

Not thirsty, she was about to refuse, but then realised that she should accept his offer as a small step forward towards developing some form of *entente cordiale* between them.

'I have a long day tomorrow, so I'd like fruit juice, if that's okay.'

He gestured for her to sit on one of the stools beneath the counter, but instead she leaned against the wall, next to an old-fashioned dresser filled with colourful ceramics which, though at odds with the sleek lines of Andreas's modern kitchen, grounded the room with their reminder of history and other lives lived.

She jumped when her phone rang again. She grabbed it off the dresser. It was Lizzie. She let the call go to her voicemail, but that didn't stop Andreas giving her a critical stare.

The cold apple juice was sharp and refreshing, and thankfully helped her refocus on the task at hand. 'So, can we talk?'

He lifted his own glass of water and took a drink, his eyes never leaving her. 'What about?'

Butterflies fluttered in her stomach at his icy tone. 'Sofia's my best friend. This wedding means the world to her. I don't want anything…or anybody…to upset her.'

'Meaning me?'

She met his gaze and a wave of protectiveness for her friend had her returning his intimidating stare with conviction. 'Yes. Sofia is marrying Christos because she loves him—not for any other reason.'

'So you said before.'

His flippancy irked her and she asked sharply, 'Why have you agreed to host the wedding here, to be best man, if you don't approve?'

He held her gaze with a steady coolness, but his jaw tightened in irritation. 'When Christos asked me to be his best man I told him my concerns. But I believe in family loyalty, so of course I agreed. It would not have been honourable to do otherwise. And as for this island—we spent our childhood summers here, and we always vowed that we would marry in the island chapel one day. I'm not going to deny Christos that wish, no matter what my misgivings are.'

He stared at her hard, as though defying her to ask any more questions. But there was something in his expression that was puzzling her. Was it a hint of wounded pride? Why did she feel as though she was missing some significant point in this conversation? Sofia had mentioned that Andreas had once been briefly married. Was he remembering his own marriage? Or was she just reading this all wrong? Grace had formed the impression from Sofia that he had easily moved on from that marriage to a string of other relationships.

She walked towards him and stopped a little distance away. She forced herself to look into his eyes. Her heart pounded at the hard cynicism she found there. 'I can understand why you might have some concerns. But Sofia is an incredible person and I truly believe they will be extremely happy together. They were made for one another. For their sake I would like us to get on.'

He moved away from the countertop. Beneath his open-necked shirt, golden skin peppered with dark hair was visible. He took a step closer to her. Her breath caught as she inhaled his scent—a sensual muskiness with hints of spice and lemon. She stared at the broadness of his shoulders beneath the slim-fitting white shirt, the narrowness of his hips in the dark tuxedo trousers, the long length of his legs.

He stepped even closer, towering over her, those light green eyes burnished with gold scorching into hers. He leaned down towards her ear and in a low growl asked, 'Tell me…will your boyfriend be joining you for the wedding?'

His voice rumbled through her body. She didn't know

whether to run away from the dark danger that everything about this man screamed or just give in and lean into the heat and invisible pull of his powerful body.

She stepped back. Again he pinned her to the spot with his demanding stare.

'I don't have a boyfriend.'

His eyes narrowed. 'Then who's Matt?'

'Matt? Matt's my brother.'

For a moment he considered her suspiciously, as though searching for the truth. Then abruptly he turned away.

'I understand from Christos that you wish to use the workshops down by the island jetty to prepare the flowers? Tomorrow my gardener Ioannis will show you the way. If you need to travel to any of the other islands Ioannis will take you. My housekeeper Eleni will take care of your meals. Your bedroom is upstairs—the third room to the right. I have left your luggage there.'

Rebelliousness surged through her at his dismissive tone. 'And what about you, Andreas? Will you have a partner at the wedding this weekend?'

He turned and considered her. 'No. I'll be on my own. The way I like it. And, to answer your earlier question, I can see no reason why we cannot get on with one another. I will go along with Christos's wishes…but please don't expect me to embrace this wedding with the same enthusiasm as you. My days of believing in romance and love are long gone.'

He threw the uneaten orange into the bin, muttered, '*Kalinichta*…goodnight…' and walked out of the room.

Grace collapsed against the wall, suddenly exhausted. She closed her eyes and prayed that tomorrow would go more smoothly. That the deliveries would arrive on time.

That in the cold light of the day her senseless attraction to Andreas would diminish.

Because Andreas Petrakis was as far removed from her ideal man as Attila the Hun.

CHAPTER TWO

ANDREAS SLOWED THE pace of his morning swim for the last hundred metres into the shore and trailed his eye up the cliff-face and the numerous terraces built into it.

In only three days' time the island would be overrun with the hundreds of guests who were to be ferried out to the island from Athens. There would be polite avoiding of his eye, curious studying of him to see if he gave any sign of remembering his own vows of commitment, and how his marriage had ended within twelve short months.

He hoped Christos knew what he was doing. That he knew Sofia as well as he said he did. Andreas did not want to see his brother hurt. Or his family humiliated and disappointed again.

He had spent the past month, since Christos had announced his engagement, avoiding any involvement in the wedding preparations. He would respect his brother's decision and play the dutiful best man. Get along with the chief bridesmaid as best he could. But he'd keep his distance from her. To do otherwise, no matter how tempting, would be foolhardy.

There was undoubtedly a spark of attraction between them, but she was an out-and-out romantic and he had no business getting involved with a woman who believed in fairy-tale endings. Not when he knew that love was nothing but a fantasy. Anyway, the best man should *never* get involved with the chief bridesmaid. It was never a good idea in the long run.

On the warm sand at the base of the cliff he grabbed his towel and made his way back up the steep steps to the villa. He had rushed into marriage, like Christos. In the intense whirlwind of infatuation he had thought he had found love. But through her lies and betrayal his ex-wife had hardened his heart for ever. He would never trust again. He had always believed in marriage, in having children. But now those were the long forgotten dreams of an innocent.

Close to the top of his climb, he came to a stop on the final steps. Laden down with files and paperwork, her hair tied up into a high ponytail, bouncing from side to side, Grace rushed down the path towards him. She was dressed in a white lace blouse, pink shorts and trainers, and the sight of her bare legs had his abdominals tensing with frustration.

She spotted him and slowed, her eyes quickly flicking over him. Heat filled her cheeks before she looked away.

'*Kalimera*—good morning, Grace.'

She ventured another quick gaze at him and nodded. This time her eyes held his.

The morning sun highlighted the honey and caramel tones in her hair, emphasising the mesmerising violet colour of her eyes. Eyes that could do funny things to a man's resolve if he wasn't careful.

Invisible strings of mutual attraction tugged tight. He wanted to step closer, to cradle the delicate exposed lines of her neck, draw her mouth up towards his...

The beads of seawater that had been slowly following a lazy path down his body now felt electrified on his unbearably sensitive skin. He felt alive to a world of sensual possibilities.

She made a few attempts to talk, all the while shuffling the files in her arms, her eyes darting to and from him.

Why was she so jumpy? 'Is everything okay?'

Her head moved almost imperceptibly from side to side, as though she was trying to weigh up how she was going to reply. She bit down on her lip, exposing the not quite perfect alignment of her front teeth, with one tooth slightly overlapping the other. Why did he find that imperfection so appealing?

Eventually she said in a rush, 'Ioannis just called. The flowers are already down at the jetty. Apparently they were delivered before dawn. The delivery company were supposed to call me. I was meant to inspect them before they left... And, worse still, they were supposed to carry them as far as the workshops for me.'

The workshops sat on a steep hill overlooking the cove—she would need some help. 'Ask Ioannis to help you.'

'He had to go to Naxos to collect the caterers and the wedding planner and her team. A florist from Naxos was supposed to be coming with them, to assist me today, but she just called to say that she's sick.'

Thee mou! Did Grace know what she was doing? A missed flight, a missed delivery, and now a sick member of staff. 'Get Ioannis and the wedding planner's team to help you when they arrive.'

'I can't leave the flowers out in this heat. I have to get them into the cool of the workshops straight away.'

Why hadn't he opted to stay in Athens for the duration of the wedding preparations? *Because you love your brother. And as his work in London has prevented him*

*from travelling until Thursday you promised to be here
in case there were any issues.*

But he had urgent business to deal with too. He didn't
have time for this. His instinct about Grace needing baby-
sitting hadn't been far off the mark after all.

'Do you usually face so many problems?'

She considered him for a brief moment, her anxiety
fading to be replaced by a sharp intelligence. 'There are
always unforeseen problems with the flowers for any
wedding. It's my job to deal with them as quickly as I
can.' She paused, and although her cheeks grew even
more enflamed she considered him with a quiet dignity.
'I'm sure *you* must experience unexpected problems all
the time in your work…and will therefore understand
why I need to ask for your help.'

'*My* help?' He had a mountain of work to do. He didn't
have time to act as some florist's assistant.

She inhaled a deep breath and answered, 'I appreciate you're probably very busy, but if you could give me
half an hour I'd be grateful.'

She awaited his response with a spirited stare of defiance, challenging him to say no. Despite himself he ad-
mired her feistiness.

Against all logic and his pledges to keep a wide berth
around the chief bridesmaid he found himself saying, 'I'll
give you half an hour. No more. First I must get changed
and reschedule a call.'

Light-headed, Grace turned away as Andreas climbed the
path up to the villa, her heart pirouetting with humiliation…and something else she didn't want to think about.

He must think she was completely incompetent.

The ground beneath her no longer felt solid. Had she
sat in the sun for too long earlier, whilst finalising her

plans for the reception flowers out on the terrace? She came to a stop and gulped down some air.

Who was she trying to kid? This had nothing to do with too much sun. Rather too much of Andreas Petrakis. Too much of his near naked body. Too much of seeing the seawater that had fallen in droplets along the hard muscles of his chest, down over a perfectly defined six-pack until they'd reached the turquoise swimming shorts that sat low on his narrow hips.

She had been right last night. He *was* a Greek god. His sleeked back hair had emphasised the prominence of his cheekbones, the arrow-straightness of his nose, the enticing fullness of his mouth. And he had a long-limbed muscular body the likes of which she had only ever seen cast in marble whilst on a school tour to the British Museum. Sofia and she had circled those statues, giddy with teenage fascination.

She would *not* turn around and take one final glimpse. No way.

Oh, what the heck?

His back was a vast golden expanse of taut muscle, from broad powerful shoulders down to those narrow hips. And she could not help but notice the firm muscles of his bottom and the long, athletic shape of his legs as he easily climbed the steep path back towards the villa.

The goofy grin on her mouth faded. Okay, so he was gorgeous, and he did very peculiar things to her heart. But she had to dig one big hole and bury that attraction. She was here to do a job. She had to act professionally. Even if the gods were determinedly working against her right now in a bid to make her appear completely clueless.

Early this morning she had thrown open her balcony doors to dazzling sunshine and the stunning vista of far-away islands floating on the azure Aegean Sea. A light breeze had curled around her like a welcoming hug to the Cyclades Islands. Only the tinkle of goat bells had been carried on the air.

That paradise she had awoken to had given her a renewed determination that she was going to enjoy every second of this trip, which was to be the start of the life of adventure she had craved for so many years. After years of being held hostage to her father's control and manipulation she was determined to be free. Free to love every second of every day, to fill her life with fun and exhilaration. Free to accomplish all her own ambitions and prove that she *did* have worth.

All of which meant that tangling with her arrogant playboy host was the last thing she should be doing. Her priority had to be the flowers. If this project went wrong she could kiss her fledgling career goodbye. And, God forgive her for her pride, she wanted to prove to Andreas that she wasn't a bumbling idiot—contrary to all current evidence.

Set into the cliff-face above the small harbour, the workshops mirrored the sugar cube style of the main house. Inside, the cool double-height rooms with their exposed roof beams and roughly plastered walls would be perfect for storing and assembling the flowers.

Grace quickly moved about the first workshop on the row, sweeping dust off benches and pulling two into the centre of the room for her to work at. Outside again, she raced down to the harbour jetty, grabbed a stack of flower buckets, and ran back up to the workshops. Within minutes her legs were burning because of the steep incline.

Back inside the workshop, she dropped the buckets to the floor and exhaled heavily. What had she taken on? How on earth was she going to strip and trim over a thousand stems of peonies and lisianthus by herself?

She gave herself a shake and scanned the room. There was no tap. What was she going to do about water? She ran into the adjoining room and almost cried in relief when she saw a sink in the far corner. She twisted the tap. The gush of water restored some calm.

Twice more she ran down to the jetty to collect the remaining buckets, and the box she had packed personally, which contained all her essential tools: knives, scissors, pruners and a vast assortment of tapes, wires and cord twine.

By the time Andreas appeared at the workshop door she was not only hot and sweaty but also covered in wet patches from the sloshing water as she carried endless buckets of water from the adjoining room back into her temporary workshop.

He, in contrast, was his usual effortlessly cool and elegant self, wearing faded denim jeans that hung low on his hips and a slim-fitting sea-green polo shirt. Muscular biceps, washboard abs... How good would it be to walk into his arms and feel the athletic strength of his body?

For a few seconds every ounce of energy drained from her and she wondered how she didn't crumble to the workshop floor in a mess of crushing attraction.

Pointedly he glanced at his exquisite platinum watch.

Inwardly she groaned at her lack of focus.

She rushed to the door and pointed down towards the jetty. The pale wooden structure sitting over the teal-blue sea was the perfect romantic setting for the arrival of the wedding guests on Saturday.

'The flowers are all packed in those large rectangular boxes, stacked together. We need to get those inside now. The other boxes can wait until later.'

She was about to pass him when he placed his hand

on her forearm. 'I'll collect the boxes—you stay here and continue with the work you were doing.'

She swallowed hard, her whole body on alert at the pleasurable sensation of his large hand wrapped around her arm. 'We don't have time.'

His eyes moved downwards and lingered on her chest.

Grace followed his gaze. And almost passed out. Her wet blouse was transparent, and clinging to her crimson-trimmed bra.

His lip curled upwards in one corner and for a moment she got a glimpse of how lethal he would be if he decided to seduce her.

'Perhaps it might be better if you stay inside for a while; Ioannis and the wedding team are due to arrive soon.'

Mortified, she twisted away, grabbed some buckets and pointedly turned and nodded in the direction of his watch. 'You'd better get going as your half an hour is ticking away. I reckon you'll struggle to get all of the boxes in by then.'

A smirk grew on his lips. 'I'll try not to break into too much of a sweat...' He paused as his eyes rested on where her wet blouse was sticking to her skin. 'Although it does have its attractions.'

Lightning bolts of lust fired through her body. He noted her wide-eyed reaction and his smirk grew even larger. She twisted around and fled next door. She could have sworn she heard him chuckle.

When she returned with the filled buckets he was gone.

Andreas returned time and time again with the long rectangular flower boxes, and each time Grace heard his footsteps approach she hightailed it into the adjoining room. Only when she realised that he had moved on to carrying in the assortment of different-sized boxes that contained the other essentials did she speak. But despite her assurances that it wasn't necessary for him to bring them in, he continued to do so.

The buckets filled and flower food added, she went about stripping and trimming the stems. With bated breath she opened the first box of peonies and found light pink Sarah Bernhardt, and in the next box the ivory-white Duchesse de Nemours. Both were as big and utterly beautiful as she had hoped, and on track to open to their full blowsy glory for Saturday.

At last *something* was going right for her.

For a moment she leaned down and inhaled the sweet scent of the flowers, closing her eyes in pleasure. She might have to stay up all night to get the prep work done, but she would manage. The flowers had to be perfect for Sofia.

She had the first box completed when Andreas brought the final boxes in. Unfairly, apart from a faint sheen of perspiration on his tanned skin, he didn't appear the least bit ruffled by all the dragging and hauling.

Hitting the timer on her smartphone, she twisted it around to show him the display. 'Thirty-six minutes, fourteen seconds.'

His mouth twitched for a few seconds before he flashed his watch at her and tapped one of the dials. 'Nineteen minutes and forty-three seconds to carry in the flowers, which was all you specified. So I win.'

'I didn't know we were competing.'

Those green eyes flashed with way too much smugness for her liking. 'Why did you time me then?'

'Oh, just curiosity.' Keen to change the subject, she added, 'I'm really grateful for your help—thank you.'

He shrugged in response and turned his attention to

the remaining stack of flower boxes, and then to the already trimmed peonies, sitting in their buckets of water. 'Why so many roses?'

'They're not roses.'

He contemplated the flowers dubiously.

She twisted the stem she was working on and held it out towards him. 'They're peonies. I thought you would have known, being Greek, as apparently they are called after Paean, who healed Hades's wounds. It's thought that they have healing properties. It's also believed that they represent a happy life...and a happy marriage.'

To that he raised a sceptical eyebrow.

With her floral shears, Grace snipped an inch diagonally off the end of the stem. 'Let me guess...you're not the type to buy flowers?'

'On occasion I have.' A grin tugged at the corner of his mouth in reaction to her quizzical glance. 'Okay, I admit that I let my PA organise the details.'

She tried to ignore how good it was to see those eyes sparkle with humour. 'Now, *that's* just cheating... I hope you at least specify what type of flowers you want to send?'

He seemed baffled at the idea. 'No—why should I?'

'Because each flower represents something. When you send a flower you are sending a message with it.'

He looked horrified at that prospect. 'Like what?'

Amused, she decided to make the most of him being on the back foot in this conversation. 'Well, new beginnings are symbolised by daffodils...a secret love is represented by gardenias...' She paused for effect before continuing, 'True love is shown by forget-me-nots, and sensuality by jasmine.'

Their eyes met and tension pulsed in the air. But then

he broke his gaze away. 'How about, *Thanks for a good night, but this is nothing serious*?'

Her heart sank. 'A yellow rose is used for friendship, if that's what you're trying to say. But maybe it would be better not to send anything on those occasions.'

Unable to bear the way his gaze had fastened on her again, she bent her head and trimmed the foliage on the stem with quick cuts, a constant mantra sounding in her brain: *Stay away from him; he's a sure-fire path to heart-break.*

He eventually spoke. 'Perhaps. But I still don't understand why so many flowers are needed for one wedding.'

So often she had heard the same incredulous question from grooms-to-be, who struggled to understand the volume of flowers needed to create a visual impact and how important flowers were for setting the mood and tone of the wedding day. She was used to talking them through her plans, and always keen to make them comfortable and happy with her designs, but with Andreas she felt even more compelled to spell out the intricacies of wedding floral design and the attention to detail required. She wanted it to be clear to him that she was not *playing with flowers*. That her presence on his island was essential.

'Eight hundred peonies. Two hundred lisianthus, to be precise. Along with the bridal party bouquets, and the flower displays that will be needed outside the chapel and on the terrace, each reception table will have a centrepiece of five vases with five peonies in each, so with twenty tables—'

'That adds up to five hundred flowers.'

'Exactly. Today I have to trim, cut and place all the stems in water. Tomorrow the stems will need to be cut again and placed in fresh water. On Friday fifty potted bay trees and storm lanterns will be delivered, to be placed along the walkway between the jetty and the chapel, and on the main terrace for the reception and the dancing.'

He surveyed the boxes of flowers yet to be opened and then looked over to the large pile of other unopened boxes. His gaze narrowed. 'What's in the other boxes?'

She had gone over her stock list so often she had no problem in recalling all the items she had ordered. 'One hundred glass vases for the centrepieces, two hundred votive candles, fifty lantern candles and thirty pillar candles. Flower foam, more string, wire, ribbon... The list goes on. They all need to be unloaded today, ready to be prepped tomorrow. And I also have to finalise my designs.'

He checked his watch and frowned. 'I have to get back to my conference calls. Is there anyone else who can help you with all this?'

'I'll manage.' Even if it meant she would be working late into the night. 'Two more florists will be joining me tomorrow, but I need to get all the basic prep done today or I'll run out of time.'

His eyes drifted over the now crowded room. 'I have to admit that I hadn't realised the volume of work involved.'

A smile tugged at her lips. 'Perhaps now you understand why I need to be here and not touring the nightclubs of Athens.'

He gave a gracious nod in response, his eyes softening in amusement. 'Yes, but that's not to say that I don't think it's all crazy.'

With that he left the room, and Grace stood stockstill for the longest while, her heart colliding against her chest at being on the receiving end of his beautiful smile.

Six hours later Andreas made his way back down to the workshops. Eleni, although tied up in an argument with the catering team over the use of her beloved pots and pans, had whispered to him that Grace had not appeared for lunch, and gestured in appeal towards a tray of food.

Never able to say no to his indomitable housekeeper, who had him wrapped around her little finger, Andreas approached the workshops now in frustration at yet another disruption to his day. But he had to admit to concern for Grace at the huge amount of work she had to tackle alone, and to a grudging respect for her determination and energy in doing so.

Inside the first workshop the tiled floor was akin to a woodland scene, with green leaves and cuttings scattered everywhere. In the middle, armed with a sweeping brush, Grace was corralling the leaves into one giant pile, her face a cloud of tension.

A quick glance about the room told him she was making slow progress. She needed help. And unfortunately he was the only person available.

'Eleni's concerned that you missed lunch.'

She jerked around at his voice.

He dropped the tray on the edge of a workbench.

'That's very kind of her.' She paused as she grabbed a nearby dustpan and composting bag. 'Please thank her for me but tell her not to worry—I can fend for myself.'

The composting bag full, Grace tied it and placed it in a corner. He, meanwhile, had taken over the scooping of the leaves.

She moved next to him, her bare legs inches from where he crouched down. If he reached out, his fingers could follow a lazy path over her creamy skin. He could learn at what point her eyes would glaze over as his fingers traced her sensitive spots. The desire to pull her down onto the mound of leaves and kiss that beautiful mouth raged inside him.

'There's no need for you to help.'

She sounded weary.

He stood. His gut tightened when he saw the exhaustion in her eyes. 'You need a break. Have some lunch. I'll finish here.'

She hesitated, but then walked over to the tray. The deep aroma of Greek coffee filled the workshop but she immediately went back to work, carrying a fresh box over to the table. In between opening the box and sorting through the flowers she hurriedly gulped down some coffee and took quick, small bites of a triangular-shaped parcel of spinach and feta cheese pie—*spanakopita*.

He gathered up the tray, ignoring her confused expression, and took it to a bench outside. When Grace joined him he said, 'You shouldn't work and eat at the same time.'

'I'm too busy.'

'Let's make a deal. If you agree to take a ten-minute break, I'll stay a while and unpack some of the supplies for you.'

She stared at him suspiciously. 'Are you sure?'

He needed to make clear his reasons for doing this. 'You're my guest—it's my duty to take care of you.'

She paused for a moment and considered his words before giving a faint nod. 'I'd appreciate your help, but I must warn you that it might prove to be a tedious job because the suppliers haven't labelled the boxes. I need you to find the glass vases for me first, as I have to prep them today. There's a box-cutter you can use on the table next to the boxes.'

He went back inside and started opening boxes. She rejoined him within five minutes. A five-minute break that had included her answering a phone call from someone called Lizzie.

A begrudging respect for her work ethic toyed with his annoyance that she hadn't adhered to her side of the bargain. He wasn't used to people going against his orders.

They both worked in silence, but the air was charged with an uncomfortable tension.

Eventually she spoke. 'What were these workshops originally used for?'

Sadness tugged in his chest at her question. He swallowed hard before he spoke. 'My uncle was a ceramicist and he built these workshops for his work.'

She rested her hands on the workbench and leaned forward. 'I noticed some ceramic pieces in your house—are they your uncle's?'

'Yes. He created them in these workshops; there's a kiln in the end room.'

'They're beautiful.'

Thrown by the admiration and excitement in her voice, he pressed his thumb against the sharp blade of the box cutter. 'He died two years ago.'

For a long while the only sound was the whistle of the light sea breeze as it swirled into the workshop.

She walked around the bench to where he was working. 'I'm sorry.'

He glanced away from the tender sincerity in her eyes. It tugged much too painfully at the empty pit in his stomach.

'What was he like?'

The centre of my world.

He went back to work, barely registering the rows of candles inside the box he had just opened.

'He was quiet, thoughtful. He loved this island. When I was a small boy the island belonged to my grandparents. They used it as their summer retreat. My uncle lived here permanently. Christos and I used to spend our summers here, free to explore without anyone telling us what to do and when to be home. That freedom was paradise. We'd swim and climb all day, and at night we'd grill fish on the beach with our uncle. He would tell us stories late into the night, trying his best to scare us with tales of sea monsters.'

'There's a gorgeous ceramic pot in the living room, with images of sea monsters and children…did he create that?'

He was taken aback that she had already noticed his single most treasured possession, and it was a while before he answered. 'Yes, the children are Christos and me.'

'What wonderful memories you both must have.'

He turned away from the beguiling softness in her violet eyes. He closed the lid of the box, still having been unable to locate the vases. It was strange to talk to someone about his uncle. Usually he closed off any conversation about him, but being here, in one of his workshops, with this quietly spoken empathetic woman, had him wanting to speak about him.

'He always encouraged me to follow my dreams, even when they were unconventional or high risk. He even funded my first ever property acquisition when I was nineteen. Thankfully I was able to pay him back with interest within a year. He believed in me, trusted me when others didn't.'

Her thumb rubbed against the corner of a box. He noticed that her nails, cut short, were varnish-free. A plaster was wrapped around her index finger and he had to stop himself from taking it in his hand.

She inhaled before she spoke. 'You were lucky to have someone like that in your life.'

Taken aback by the loneliness in her voice, he could only agree. 'Yes.'

She gave him a sad smile. 'Kasas is a very special place…you're lucky to have a house somewhere so magical.'

Old memories came back with a vengeance. 'Some people would hate it.'

'Hate this island? I think it's the most beautiful place I have ever visited.'

Andreas watched her, disarmed by the passion in her voice. He wanted to believe everything she said was heartfelt and genuine. That he wasn't being manipulated by a woman again. But cold logic told him not to buy any of it.

It was time to move this conversation on. It was getting way too personal.

'The vases aren't here.'

Her mouth dropped open and she visibly paled. 'They *have* to be.'

'I've double-checked each box—they're not.'

She gave a low groan and rushed over to the boxes, while frantically pushing buttons on her phone. As she ransacked the boxes she spoke to someone called Jan.

Andreas walked away and into the adjoining room. Once again he tried to ignore the loneliness crowding his chest at being in these workshops for the first time since his uncle had died.

A few minutes later Grace followed him into the end room, where the kiln was located. She stopped at the doorway and clenched her phone tight in her palm. Her paleness had now been replaced by a slash of red on her cheeks.

She spoke in a low voice, her eyes wary. 'The vases were never despatched by the suppliers in Amsterdam; they won't get here before Saturday.'

He had guessed as much. He gestured to the vast array

of white porcelain pots on the bench beside the kiln. 'You can use these instead.'

Her eyes grew wide and she went and picked one up. And then another. Her fingers traced over the smooth delicate ceramic. 'Are you sure?'

'He had moved back to working predominantly with porcelain in the year before he died. I've never known what to do with all his work, I didn't want to sell it...' Unexpected emotion cut off the rest of what he had been about to say.

Soft violet eyes held his. 'This can't be easy for you.'

He glanced away. 'He would like it that his work is being used for Christos's wedding.'

With that he walked back to the main workshop, wanting to put some distance between him and this woman who kept unbalancing his equilibrium. Frustration rolled through him. What was it about Grace that made him break all his own rules?

He had another ten minutes before he had to leave. There were a few small boxes yet to open.

He unwrapped a small rectangular parcel first, and found inside, wrapped in a soft cloth, a pair of silver sandals. 'These are unusual florist's supplies.'

'My sandals!' She dropped the flowers she was working on and took the slender sexy heels from him.

Imagining Grace's enticing legs in the sandals, he felt his blood pressure skyrocket. In need of distraction, he went back to opening the next box.

'The shop didn't have them in my size so I had them delivered here...' Her voice trailed off and then she said in a low, desperate voice, 'Don't open that box.'

But she was too late. His fingers were already looped around two pale pink silk straps. He lifted the material to reveal a sheer lace bustier.

With an expression of absolute mortification Grace stared at the bustier, and then down at the scrap of erotic pink lace still left in the box, sitting on a bed of black tissue paper. Odds on it was the matching panties. Red-hot blood coursed through his body.

'Yours, I take it?'

For a moment her mouth opened and closed, but then she grabbed the bustier and the box and walked away.

She kept her back to him as she bundled the bustier back into its box. 'It's for the wedding, but I'm not sure I'll wear it.'

Time for him to leave—before he burst a blood vessel. 'I have afternoon calls I have to get back to.' He made it as far as the door before he turned back. 'Grace?'

She turned around towards him.

'Wear it.'

He walked away as her lips parted in surprise. He had never wanted to grab a woman and kiss her senseless more in all his life.

CHAPTER THREE

GRACE REACHED FOR the bell clapper, feeling the ladder wobbling beneath her.

'What in the name of the devil are you doing?'

She jerked at the sound of Andreas's irate voice beneath her and the precarious ladder swayed wildly. A startled yelp from deep within her shot out into the evening air, but mercifully the ladder was steadied before it toppled to the ground.

She dared a quick glance down. A livid Andreas was gripping the side bars, one foot on the bottom rung.

She swallowed hard, uncertain as to what was more daunting: this fury, or the heat in his eyes earlier when he had lifted up her bustier. Heat that had ignited a yearning in her that had left her breathless and just plain exasperated. They didn't even particularly *like* each other. Why, then, did she feel as though she was about to combust any time she came into contact with him?

'I've decided that the chapel needs some extra decoration in addition to what I'd planned, so I'm making a garland that will hang from the bell tower down to the ground. I need to measure the exact length.'

'*Aman!* You are breaking my nerves! You shouldn't be doing this alone; the flagstones are too uneven.'

He was right, but she wasn't going to admit it. 'I'm

fine—it's a quick job.' To prove her point she knotted twine around the bell clapper and then dropped the twine spool to the ground before climbing down the ladder. She avoided looking at him and instead pulled the twine out to the angle she wanted the garland positioned at on the wedding day. Cutting it to the desired length, she ignored his infuriated expression. 'I need to climb back up and untie the other end.'

He gave an exasperated sigh and scaled the ladder himself, dropping the twine when he'd untied it. Back on the ground, he unlocked the extension ladder she had borrowed from Ioannis and collapsed it down.

Then he studied her with incensed eyes, his mouth a thin line. 'Don't try that again.'

Of course she would. But she wasn't going to get into an argument with him. 'Was there something you wanted?'

His gaze narrowed. The uncomfortable sensation that he could see right through her had her grabbing the twine off the ground and asking, 'Is it okay if I use some of the rosemary and bay growing on the terraces for the garland?'

He considered the long length of twine sceptically. 'Is it really necessary? I thought you were under pressure timewise?'

She was, but it was these final touches that would make her work stand apart. 'I'll find the time.' She paused and gestured around her. 'I want the flowers to do justice to this setting.'

Set on a rocky promenade beyond the golden sandy beach, the tiny whitewashed chapel with its blue dome had a dramatic backdrop of endless deep blue seas and skies.

His jaw hardened even more, and she winced to think about the pressure his poor teeth must be under.

'My guess is that Sofia would prefer her bridesmaid *not* to be in a plaster cast on her wedding day for the sake of a few flowers.'

Wow, that was a low blow. 'If you'll excuse me? I need to finalise my plans for the chapel's bespoke floral arrangements—or, as you call them, "a few flowers".'

His mouth twisted at her barbed comment. 'It will be dark soon.'

'I won't be long.' When he didn't move, she added, 'You don't need to wait for me.'

'And have you getting lost on the way back? No, thanks. I don't want to have to spend a second night rescuing you.'

With that he turned and went and sat on the low white-washed wall that surrounded the chapel terrace.

Behind him the deep blue sea met the purple evening sky; it was a postcard-perfect image of the Greek Islands but for the scowling man who dominated the frame.

Grace circled the terrace outside the chapel, all the while taking notes, scribbling into her notebook. Every now and again she would glance in his direction and throw him a dirty glare. Which he was just fine with. Because he was in a pretty dirty mood himself. In every sense.

All afternoon he had been plagued with images of her wearing that sexy lingerie. The bustier hugging her small waist, lifting her breasts to a height and plumpness that demanded a man taste them. Those skimpy panties moulded to her pert bottom... Hell, he couldn't go there again. His call to the Cayman Island planners had been a washout as a result.

She had already put in a twelve-hour day, with less

than five minutes taken for lunch. Did it *really* matter this much what the flowers looked like? Did anyone even *notice* the flowers on a wedding day?

'Why does this wedding mean so much to you?'

She turned to him in surprise, her notebook falling to her side. The long length of her golden ponytail curled over one shoulder and his fingers tingled in remembrance of its softness and her delicate sensual scent last night. His gut tightened. Those legs were once again driving him crazy with images of the chief bridesmaid that he certainly shouldn't be thinking of.

He dated some of the most beautiful women in Athens. Why was he so drawn to this out-of-bounds woman?

Eventually she walked over and sat on the wall beside him. She left a significant gap between them.

'I first met Sofia in our local playground when we were both four. A boy had pushed me off the top of the fire pole. Sofia marched right over and kicked him in the shin before helping me up.' She gave an amused shrug. 'We've never looked back since then. We went to the same primary and secondary school…and we were supposed to go to university together…' She paused and gave a small sigh. 'But that didn't work out for me. After years of coming to school concerts with me, and wet Saturday afternoons standing at the side of a freezing cold soccer pitch, I owe Sofia big-time.'

'I don't understand? Why were you going to school concerts together for years?'

Her lips twisted for a moment before she distractedly rubbed a hand along the smooth skin of her calf. 'My parents weren't always available, so I used to go to Matt's football matches and my younger sister Lizzie's school events. Sofia used to come to keep me company. Even though she could have been off doing something much more entertaining than listening to a school orchestra murdering some piece of music.'

He considered what she'd said. Maybe Christos *was* marrying a good woman.

As though to emphasise that point, Grace studied him coolly. 'Christos is a very lucky man. He's marrying an incredible woman—smart and loving.'

'It sounds like he is.'

A small note of triumph registered in her eyes. 'So, can we agree that we will do everything to make this wedding as special a day as possible for them?'

He wanted to say yes, but the word just wouldn't come. He still feared that Christos might regret his haste in years to come. As he did. So instead he said, 'You're one of life's hopeless romantics, aren't you?'

Those astounding violet eyes narrowed and she leaned away from him as she considered his words. 'Romantic, yes—hopeless, no. I'm not ashamed to admit that I believe in love...in marriage. I see it all the time in my work, and with Sofia and Christos. It's the most wonderful thing that exists.'

'Have *you* ever been in love?'

Her shoulders jerked at his question. 'No.'

'But you want to be?'

An unconscious smile broke on her lips, and her eyes shone with dreams. 'Yes. And I'm greedy... I want it all. I want love at first sight, the whirlwind, the marriage, the children, the growing old together. The perfect man.'

He'd once thought life was that simple. In exasperation, he demanded, 'The perfect man...? What on earth is *that*?'

'A man who will sweep me off my feet, who will make life fun and exciting. A man who believes in love too. In kindness and tenderness.'

For a moment she eyed what must be his appalled expression, given the angry frown that had popped up on her brow. And then, as though his reaction had unlocked something inside of her, she let go with all barrels firing.

'A man who's intelligent, honourable, loyal…and great in bed.'

He tried not to laugh at how disconcerted she seemed by her own last statement. Clearing his throat, he said, 'Wow, that's some guy. But I hate to break it to you… that's not reality. Love is complex and messy and full of disappointment. Not like the fairy tale and the X-rated Prince Charming you've just described. Do you *really* believe someone like that exists?'

Solemn eyes met his. 'I hope so.' Then a hint of fear, maybe doubt, clouded her eyes. For a few moments they sat in silence, until she asked, 'How about you?'

For a while he just stared at her—at the high, slanting cheekbones, the freckle-sized birthmark just below her right ear, surprised by her naivety…by her optimism. In truth, a part of him was wildly envious of that.

'As I said last night, I have no interest in love—in relationships full-stop.'

'Why?'

Even if he'd wanted to, even if he'd trusted Grace he wouldn't be able to find adequate words to describe the mess his marriage had descended into.

'I'd rather not talk about it.'

Disappointment filled her eyes. But then she gave him a sympathetic smile and he instantly realised that she already knew about his marriage. Christos must have said something. Just how much *did* she know? Anger flared inside him. He did not want her sympathy. He did not need the humiliation of her pity.

She shifted on the wall and gazed at him uncertainly. 'Sofia mentioned that you were once married...'

He didn't respond, but raised a questioning eyebrow instead, waiting for her to continue.

She gestured towards the chapel. 'Having the ceremony in the same chapel...' She trailed off.

His heart sank. He really didn't want to talk about this. 'I didn't marry here.'

'Oh.' Clearly flustered by his answer, she muttered, 'Sorry, I assumed you had. After what you said last night about Christos and you always wanting to marry here.'

With an impatient sigh, he answered, 'My ex wanted to get married in Athens.'

She digested this for some time before she asked, 'Did you mind not marrying here?'

At the time he *had* minded. But his ex had been determined from day one that theirs would be *the* society wedding of the year in Athens, and had used his uncle's recent death to persuade him not to marry on the island. She had insisted that he would find it too upsetting to be surrounded by reminders of him on their wedding day.

It had all been lies. In the bitter arguments after he had confronted her with the photos of her with her lover she had admitted as much. His one consolation from the entire debacle was that at least the island wasn't tainted with memories of the worst decision of his life. His biggest failure.

He waited for a few minutes before he spoke, afraid of the anger that might spill out otherwise. 'It doesn't matter; it's in the past.'

'I'm sorry your marriage didn't work out. It must have been a difficult time,' she said quietly.

Disconcerted, Andreas could only stare at her. Was she really the first person who had said such a thing to him? Everyone else had been caught up in outrage at his ex's behaviour, or too embarrassed to say anything. No one—probably in the face of his anger and defiance—had dared to acknowledge just how difficult it had been for him.

His pride demanded that he just shrug off her comments, and he was about to do so when she gave him a glance of understanding that totally disarmed him.

Reluctantly he acknowledged, 'It *was* difficult.'

'You never know—you might find happiness in the future with someone else.'

Not her too. 'Please tell me that you're not one of those women who believe they can change a man…make him fall in love.'

At first she stared at him with a stunned expression, but then her eyes grew hard and cold. 'Andreas, I've had a lifetime's worth of arguments and fights, endless disappointments at failing to get a man to love me. The idea of getting into a relationship with a man who doesn't believe in love or have the capacity to love—for whatever reason—would be my idea of hell. And, trust me, I'm no martyr.'

What was she talking about? Had some guy messed her around?

He tried to remain calm when he spoke again. 'Who were you fighting with?'

Her shoulders dropped and she ran a hand tiredly down over her face. With a heavy sigh, she said, 'How about we get a drink.'

A little while later they sat outside on the main terrace of the villa, with the setting sun disappearing behind the horizon in a blaze of fiery pinks on the purple sky. Along with white wine, Andreas had brought to the table a supper of cheese pie—*tiropita*—freshly baked by Eleni that afternoon, and a bowl of Greek salad.

The filo pastry and salty feta cheese of the *tiropita* melted in her mouth, but she was unable to eat more than a few bites in the silence that had settled between them since returning from the chapel.

Her gaze met his and her stomach clenched at the thought of having to recount her past. She took a sip of wine and pushed back into her chair, squeezing her hands tight in her lap. This trip was supposed to be the start of her new life. She didn't want to remember the past. But she wanted to explain why she would never try to force a man to love her. That despite the attraction between them, and Andreas's obvious thoughts to the contrary, she wanted nothing from him.

'When I was seventeen my mum left us. My brother Matt was twelve, my sister Lizzie fourteen. I was due to go to university that year, but I couldn't leave Matt and Lizzie.'

'Why?'

Memories of standing outside her mother's isolated cottage in Scotland, trying to build up the courage to knock, swamped her. The humiliation of begging her mum to allow Matt and Lizzie to go and live with her only for her to refuse.

'My father...'

This was so hard. Should she say nothing? What *could* she say about her father? Would Andreas even understand? After all he was a driven businessman too. Was he as motivated by money and power as her father? Had that ambition caused his marriage to collapse? Despondency washed over her at the thought that that might have been the case. She suddenly had to know if he was like her father.

'What's the most important thing in your life?'

He considered her warily. 'Why do you ask?'

'I'll explain in a little while.'

For a moment she thought he wouldn't give her an answer. Then, 'Without a doubt my family: Christos, my mother.' He paused before he added, 'My father.'

She searched his eyes but he looked away. Though she had only met his father once, at the engagement party, she had quickly formed the impression that he was impatient and brusque—the type of man who would proudly boast that he didn't suffer fools gladly, with no comprehension of just how foolish and shortsighted that comment was.

In a quiet voice she asked, 'Don't you get on? You and your father?'

'It's not the easiest of relationships.'

Why was he so closed? He told her so little about himself. But then maybe he would understand if he too had a difficult relationship with his father.

'With my father, his business is the only thing that matters. Family never features in his priorities. After my mother left, it was down to me to care for Matt and Lizzie. He didn't care. Though we could barely afford it, he wanted to send them away to boarding school. They were both devastated after my mum left. They needed love and comforting, not some impersonal school.'

Apart from Sofia, she had never confided any of this to another person. Vulnerability and embarrassment sat in her throat like a double-vice grip and she studied the terrace table, bewildered by just how upset she felt. Questioning the sense in telling him all of this. Inadequacy washed over her—so ferocious she thought she might drown.

'Are you okay?'

She peeped up and nodded. Her heart slammed to a stop when she saw the gentleness in his eyes.

'You gave up university to stay with your brother and sister; that's very admirable.'

She swallowed against the emotion lodged in her throat and said, 'I thought that I might be able to get my dad to love Matt and Lizzie, to see how much they needed him. But I just couldn't get through to him. I spent years trying to make things perfect, until I realised that there was no point. After that my objective was to get them to university...away from him. Matt started university this year; Lizzie's in her third year. They're both happy and settled.'

'And what about you?'

'I left home last year, at the same time as Matt. I'm hoping I'll be able to buy an apartment soon—one that can be a home for us all. I've always dreamt of being a florist, and for the past few years, while I've studied floristry at night, I've worked with a wedding floral designer at the weekends. Since I left home I've worked as a florist full-time. After this wedding I'm going freelance as a wedding floral designer, and at some point hopefully I'll be able to open my own flower shop too.'

'Why floristry?'

Was that a note of disapproval in his voice? Compared to his success, her dreams must seem so insignificant.

She glanced at him sharply and asked, 'Why do you ask?'

'Out of curiosity...' He considered her for a while, and then with a grin he added, 'And I reckon the best man and the chief bridesmaid should know a little about each other.'

Grace eyed him suspiciously. 'Have we just taken a step forward in peace negotiations?'

He flashed her a wicked grin that almost had her falling off her chair. 'Perhaps. And, for the record, my question wasn't a criticism.'

'Sorry—it's just that you sounded like my dad. He thinks a career in floristry is a dead end.'

'Why would he say that?'

'Because there's little monetary gain to be made in it as a career—certainly not the sort of wealth *he* admires anyway. I worked in my father's business when I left school. He wanted me to stay and take over the logistics department. He even offered to give me a percentage share in the firm to stay.'

'You weren't tempted by his offer?'

'Not for a minute. It was just his way of trying to keep me in his control.'

He looked into the distance and scowled. 'Emotional blackmail.'

She felt something unlock within her at knowing that he understood. 'Yes.'

He gazed at her for a while and an invisible bond stretched between them.

He broke his gaze. 'So, why floristry?'

'I love everything about flowers—their scent, texture, colours. It's challenging to create a beautiful bouquet or a centrepiece, but so much fun too, especially for weddings, which are such happy affairs.'

'I'm impressed that you've taken on *this* wedding. I'm guessing it's a big project for someone relatively new to the business?'

Her doubts and fears about messing up came charging back and she didn't know how to respond as her heart thudded in her chest. She gave a shrug that belied the butterflies soaring in her belly. 'I'm aiming high...

I just hope I don't crash back down to earth in a blaze of bad publicity.'

'That won't happen—not with the amount of prep and planning you've done.'

'I hope so. It's really important to me that my flowers do justice to Sofia and Christos's love and the vows they will be taking.'

'Why did you choose to specialise in weddings? I would have thought they are particularly demanding?'

'They are—but I love pushing myself to design something new and unique for each couple and the time pressures involved. People in love are full of wonder and optimism, and they are usually thrilled with the work you do... What better clients could anyone wish for? I had years of my father's hardness and cynicism. I want to do something that's fun and positive now. I want to live in a world where people care about one another, where there is kindness and respect. Does that sound crazy to you?'

He contemplated her words thoughtfully before eventually saying, 'Perhaps, but it's a nice dream. And to me it sounds like you already show a lot of kindness and care towards your siblings.'

'I try to be there for them as much as I can.'

'Is that why you've never travelled alone before?'

'Up to now I could never go without them. We couldn't afford to travel much, but when we did it was all three of us together—sometimes Sofia came too.'

'They call and text you a lot. Do you still feel responsible for them?'

It wasn't something she had thought about before. 'I suppose I do.'

'Maybe you need to let them go a little in order to focus on your own future.'

Everything in Grace recoiled at what he said. She didn't want to talk about this. She had a duty to them.

She pushed away the uneasy thought that he was possibly right.

'It's not as easy as that.'

Grace stood quickly and began to clear their plates. She kept her eyes low, refusing to look at him.

'I didn't mean to upset you.'

She studied him cautiously. 'It's okay.' She eyed him again for a moment before giving a heavy sigh. 'Anyway, you're not the only one who might say the wrong thing sometimes. I'm sorry if my enthusiasm for the wedding is over the top at times. I should realise not everyone is a wedding freak like I am.'

For a moment he considered challenging her on the fact that what he'd said might not be the wrong thing to point out, but her guarded expression told him to back off. So instead he said, with a smile, 'Wedding freak—that's a new term for me.'

She lowered the dishes in her hands to the table again. 'Thank you for your help today.'

Genuine gratitude shone from her eyes and he was taken aback at how good it felt to be appreciated, to know that he had helped. When had he stopped helping others? Closed himself off from the world?

He was thankfully pulled out of the uncomfortable realisation when she spoke again. 'I realise you must be very busy with your work. I'm sorry if I caused any disruption.'

He tipped back in his chair and scratched the back of his head ruefully. 'I must admit that the contents of that last box affected my concentration all afternoon.'

She gave a nervous smile and hurriedly picked up the

dishes again. 'I'm going in to get a sweater. Is it okay if I get some coffee at the same time?'

'Use the kitchen as you wish.'

'Would you like one too?'

He nodded his acceptance and as she walked away he turned in his chair, his eyes sweeping over the sway of her hips, the pertness of her bottom. She had changed when they'd got back from the chapel, into jeans and a close-fitting baby blue tee shirt that showed the curves of her full, high breasts to perfection.

Damn it, but he was deeply attracted to her. He wanted to hold her and feel those soft lips under his, to touch the plumpness of her bottom, run his thumb along the outline of her breasts.

Aman! This was madness.

Grace wanted love and fairy-tale endings. He couldn't give her either. Being burnt in love, humiliated, was an experience he was never going to repeat. Anyway, this woman who had selflessly raised her siblings and opened up to him so honestly tonight, exposing her tender and honourable nature, deserved more than a short, superficial affair.

He glanced at his watch. She had been gone for well over ten minutes. Was everything okay? Had he upset her more than he'd thought?

He stood and walked out of the alcove in which the terrace table sat, heading towards the kitchen.

In the shadows of the curve of the alcove wall he ran straight into her, their bodies colliding hard. She jerked backwards and he grabbed hold of her as she stumbled. She trembled beneath his fingers.

Disquiet coursed through him. 'Are you okay? Has something happened?'

'I'm fine. I just can't find my sweater. I thought I'd left it in the kitchen this morning.'

She spoke in a low, breathless whisper, and he stepped even closer to her and lowered his head. This close, he could feel the heat of her body. The darkness enveloped them, heightening his awareness of her, of the heat of her body, her sweet floral scent, the smoothness of her skin beneath his fingers, the delicate curve of her arm. He wanted to pull her towards him, to feel her body crushed against his.

His voice was ragged when he spoke. 'Eleni probably moved it…you can borrow one of mine instead.'

She swayed slightly towards him, as though she too was overwhelmed by the need to get closer. He leaned forward in response, their bodies doing a private dance in which neither of them had any say.

He heard her inhale, quickly and deeply. 'No. It's fine. I should just go to bed. I'm feeling tired.'

The thought of Grace and bed had him closing his eyes in despair. He should step away. Now. But with her hair still swept up in that ponytail the delicate column of her neck proved too much of a temptation, and his fingers moved up to caress her soft exposed skin.

She gave a tiny moan and arched her neck. 'I really should go to bed.'

'Yes, you should.'

But neither of them moved.

This couldn't go on. If they didn't say goodnight soon he was going to kiss her.

Desire clogged his brain, but he managed to force out some words. 'We need to be careful.'

'Yes, of course.' She said the right thing, but her low, breathless whisper spoke of nothing but attraction and yearning.

Regret seeped into his bones but he forced himself to say, 'We need to remember that we have years of meeting again because of our ties with Christos and Sofia.'

There was a pause as she registered what he was saying. 'Okay.' She inhaled a shaky breath and took a slight step backwards. 'All the more reason why we need to learn to get on.'

'Yes, and not complicate things between us.'

She cleared her throat and stepped even further back. 'That's sensible.'

He forced himself to be blunt. 'I'm not interested in a relationship; I can't offer you anything.'

She jerked ever so slightly, and for a moment a wounded expression flickered in her eyes, pulled at her mouth. But it was quickly replaced with a proud anger.

'I don't want anything from you.'

He took a step back himself and inhaled a deep breath. '*Kalinichta*. Goodnight, Grace.'

For a few seconds she didn't move, but then she gave a quick nod and turned away.

He leaned back against the alcove wall with a groan. Yes, it was sensible not to complicate things. But sometimes *sensible* hadn't a hope in hell of stopping things getting out of control.

CHAPTER FOUR

THE FOLLOWING AFTERNOON, alone in the workshop, Grace's back ached and her stomach constantly rumbled in protest at not having been fed since dawn. But at least now she was working in the silence of siesta time, which was a welcome reprieve after the frantic pace of the morning.

She plucked up some more rosemary and bay stems and wrapped florist's wire around their base to form a neat and fragrant bundle.

Footsteps approached, at first faint, but then she heard that distinctive stride, with its quick double heel tap on every second step. For a moment they faltered outside, but then quickly climbed the stone steps up to the workshop.

She ducked her head and busied herself with another bundle of herbs, cross with the giddy anticipation that exploded in every cell of her body. She was *not* going to blush. She was *not* going to remember how close they had come to kissing last night and how she had later tossed and turned, tormented with images of beads of seawater dripping down over his taut golden stomach and disappearing beneath his turquoise shorts as they had yesterday morning.

'You're alone.'

Dressed in slim light grey trousers and an open-neck

white shirt, his suit jacket thrown over one shoulder, Andreas stood in the doorway, a hand on his narrow hip.

Why did her heart have to go bananas every time she saw him?

'The other florists have returned to Naxos with the wedding team for siesta. They'll be back later this afternoon.'

This was a detail she stupidly hadn't factored into her plans.

She inhaled a deep breath and decided to change the subject. 'You look like you're going somewhere.'

'I'm returning, in fact. I had a lunch date on Naxos.'

Her head shot up as Sofia's description of Andreas's busy love-life echoed. She gave a wobbly smile, her chest weighed down with disappointment. 'I hope it was enjoyable.'

His gaze narrowed and he walked towards her bench. She wound wire around a new bunch of herbs but almost strangled them in the process. When he didn't speak she eventually looked up at him, frustration now singing in her veins, along with a stomach-clenching sense of dejection.

Dark, serious eyes met hers. 'It was with my lawyer.'

'Oh.' Heat exploded in her cheeks.

She exhaled in relief when he walked away, but tensed when he went to stand in front of her project plans and designs for the wedding day, which she had hung on the wall earlier in order to brief the other florists. She should have taken them down again.

His back still to her, he asked, 'Aren't you having a break? Lunch? A siesta?'

The idea of lying in a darkened room with him had her glancing away from the messy sexiness of his hair, from the mesmerising triangle of the broad width of his shoulders and his narrow hips. 'I can't. I'm already hours behind with my timetable.'

He continued to stare at the plans and her stomach did a nervous roll. What if he didn't like them? Goosebumps of vulnerability popped up on her skin.

When he moved she quickly gazed back at the sad-looking herbs and began to unwind the wire. Maybe she'd be able to rescue them; it wasn't their fault, after all, that she had no sense.

He placed his jacket down on the end of the bench. 'Show me what to do.'

No! He couldn't stay. Her already shot nerves couldn't take it. Nor her pride. 'There's no need.'

'One thing you need to learn about me Grace, is that I don't say things lightly. And I don't make an offer twice.'

'That's two things.'

At first he frowned, but then a grin broke on his lips. His eyes danced mischievously, defying her to say no again to his offer.

Oh, what the heck? She needed all the help she could get.

She gestured to the bench behind her. 'I'm working on the garland for the chapel that I measured out last night. At this bench I'm assembling bunches of herbs, which I will then attach to the twine roping.'

She cut a length of the wire and showed him the required length, to which he nodded.

Then she picked up the herbs and said, 'Take three stems each of rosemary and bay and create a bunch by wrapping the wire around the bottom of the stem.'

He messed up the first bunch, tying the wire too loosely, but within a short few minutes he had picked up on the technique needed.

They worked in silence and she forced herself to

breathe normally. Well, as normally as her adrenaline-soaked body would allow. This was all so strange. Andreas Petrakis, one of the most powerful men in Greece, was standing before her, tying bunches of herbs.

'Why are you so nervous?'

'I'm not!'

He gave her a lazy, incredulous stare.

'I'm not nervous—why should I be?'

He gave a light shrug and went back to work.

'I want this to be right for Sofia.'

For a moment she paused as anxiety steamrollered up through her body, blocking her lungs and throat. She swallowed hard to push the anxiety back down into her tummy, where it nowadays permanently resided.

'But, let's face it, most of Greek society are coming to this wedding—along with various well-connected friends of Sofia and Christos from England. If I mess this up I can kiss my career ambitions goodbye. I'll never be taken seriously as a floral designer.'

He gestured towards the long line of sketches and plans on the wall. 'You have this under control. Of course you're not going to mess up. You're worrying unnecessarily—relax a little.'

Tiredness and frustration rolled through her. 'That's easy for you to say, with *your* success and *your* background.'

Taken aback by her own words, she inhaled deeply. Andreas stared at her, clearly annoyed.

She closed her eyes for a second, abhorring her own behaviour. 'I'm sorry, that was uncalled for.'

'Then why say it?'

His tone said he wasn't about to accept her apology quickly.

Embarrassment and a growing sense of panic that she

didn't have things under control had her saying in a rush, 'Because sometimes I feel so damn inadequate.'

For the longest while they stood in silence. His eyes fixed on hers until humiliation had her glancing away.

'Why inadequate?'

His tone was gentle and she gazed back in surprise. Something unlocked in her at the concern in his eyes, and she spoke in a rush, with all the insecurities tied down inside her for so long launching out of her like heat-seeking missiles.

'I left school early…didn't go to university. I'm not from a particularly wealthy background… I don't understand a lot of the nuances of social behaviour with those who are. I've probably bitten off more than I can chew with this wedding. And as I'm also the chief bridesmaid I'll hear directly any unpleasant comments people make about the flowers.'

For a moment she paused, and then she threw up her hands. A sprig of rosemary from the bundle in her hand worked loose and arced through the air. 'I've no idea why I just told you all of that…but, trust me, I know just how pathetic it sounds. There's no need for you to say anything.'

'You're wrong. There's a lot I need to say.'

She blanched at his grave tone. What had she done? Why couldn't she have kept her mouth shut?

'You're a talented and committed florist, and a good friend determined to give her best friend an incredible wedding day. So what if you didn't go to university? You were caring for your family. And, believe me, coming from a wealthy background doesn't guarantee any advantage for getting through life.'

He leaned forward on the workbench and moved closer to her, his eyes swallowing her up.

'Why do you think you're inadequate? Why do you think people would pass comment on the flowers?'

His voice was low and calm. Its quiet strength made her feel even more vulnerable and exposed. She was used to arguments and threats. Not this gentleness.

With a flippant shrug she said, 'Maybe I've been hanging around my father too long.'

'Meaning...?'

She gritted her teeth. 'My father trusts no one—including me. At work and at home he questioned everything I did, every decision I took. When I was younger I tried to stand up to him, but he would only take it out on Matt and Lizzie...grounding them, dragging them from their beds late at night because we hadn't tidied the house to his satisfaction. Calling them a useless waste of space.'

Andreas picked up a bunch of herbs from the table and plucked at the leaves. The sweetness of rosemary infused the air. His tone was anything but sweet when he spoke, 'Was there nowhere you could go? Why did you stay?'

She winced at his questions. Anger and guilt had her saying bitterly, 'Do you honestly think I would have stayed if I'd had a choice? I was *seventeen*, Andreas. I had no money... Even when I started working there was no way I was going to be able to support myself and Matt and Lizzie. I only took the job with my dad because he offered the best pay. Of course it was his way of controlling me, but I thought I would be able to save enough to move out. But rental costs just kept increasing. We have an aunt who lives in Newcastle, in the North of England, but she has her own family to care for. Anyway, Matt and Lizzie loved their school and their friends. I couldn't take them away from all that.'

He leaned even further over the workbench, resting his hand lightly on hers. When she started his hand enclosed hers, preventing her from jerking away. 'I wasn't blaming you. And you need to realise that you're *not* inadequate.'

She gave him a weak smile and tried to pull away, but his grip tightened.

He scrutinised her with a playful but determined focus. 'Say it for me—that you're not inadequate.'

'Andreas, please…'

'*Say* it.'

Though she squirmed and shook her head in exasperation she eventually gave in. 'Okay, I'll say it. I'm…' She cleared her throat as her chest tightened painfully, thick with emotions she didn't understand. 'I'm not inadequate.'

He gave a satisfied nod. His eyes, deep green pools, flickered with gold, held hers, and her heart thumped frantically.

'Shall I tell you what you *are*? *Ise poli glikos*. You are very sweet, you're loyal, determined and kind, and… very beautiful. A woman with an incredible future in front of her.'

They were the nicest words anyone had ever said to her. And she was totally unable to handle them. Flummoxed, she blushed deeply and said quietly, 'I hope so.'

'And you don't need any man or romance to complete you.'

He was wrong. She *did* need love and romance. Only love would ease the gut-wrenching loneliness that was slowly eating away at her. But she could never explain that to a man so against everything she craved.

'Perhaps, but even you have to admit that it would make life a lot more fun.'

He gave her a light look of warning. 'Be careful what you wish for.'

They worked in silence for the next half an hour, the

pile of bunched herbs between them growing ever larger. Grace tried to maintain a veneer of outward calm, but inside she was a turmoil of emotions: disbelief yet toe-tingling pleasure that he had called her beautiful, regret that he was so against love.

In the end he downed tools with a heavy sigh. 'I can't stand here listening to your stomach rumble any longer. I'm going to get you some food.' He paused to grab his jacket and muttered, almost to himself, 'And then I must tackle my best man's speech.'

Once he had left she carried the completed bunches to the other table and began attaching them to the doubled-up rope twine, creating lush foliage into which she would later place peonies encased in water tubes.

Her hands trembled. He was right. She needed food. And she needed her head examined for saying what she had. So much for staying away from each other. The man was in charge of a multinational empire. He didn't have time to be listening to her.

And yet, even though it had been hard to say what she had, it had felt right. It had been strangely freeing to see his absolute acceptance of what she'd said. None of the doubtful looks or the disinterest that had greeted her in the past when she tried to speak to other family members about her problems with her dad.

Later that evening, Andreas cursed when he reviewed the most recent budget estimates for his Cayman Islands development. The delay in planning was costing them dearly. He would have to bang some heads together to get the outstanding issues resolved. A conference call was scheduled for tonight, with all the key stakeholders. The call would not end until he was satisfied that every single issue was ironed out.

He'd need to have his wits about him for the meeting; the local contractor they were partnering with had a habit of promising the world but delivering very little substantive progress. But this damn wedding was sucking away all his usual focus. For the past few hours he'd had the distraction of the wedding planner and her team outside his window, arguing about the positioning of the reception tables. Then Grace had arrived and she and the planner had locked horns over where the flower displays would be positioned.

Grace. He had to stop thinking about her. Why was she getting under his skin so much? Earlier, she had spoken with such searing honesty he had wanted to take her in his arms and hold her. He was losing his mind.

He propped his elbows on the desk and with his eyes closed massaged his temples. His neck felt like a steel rod.

He made a low groan at the base of his throat when memories of last night returned. Her light floral scent... her skin soft and inviting when he had cradled her neck... What would it be like to trail his hand down further, unbutton her blouse, touch the enticing swell of her high and rounded breasts?

'Are you meditating or asleep?'

He leapt in his seat and let out a curse.

Grace gave a much too sexy giggle in response to his shock.

His disorientation became even more intense when he realised she was freshly showered, her hair still damp, tied up into a messy knot. She had changed into a short-sleeved denim dress that stopped a few inches above her knee and had enticing buttons running the length of it. The top three buttons were undone to reveal the cleavage he had just been fantasising about.

He had allowed physical attraction to override his common sense once before; he wouldn't let it happen again. He would need to keep this conversation short and snappy.

He leaned back in his chair. 'Neither. I was cursing whoever decided that speeches at weddings were a good idea.'

'Have you finished it?'

To that he gave a light laugh, but inside his stomach recoiled. He gestured to the paperwork piled on his desk. 'I need to deal with this first.' He didn't bother to mention his many failed attempts at writing a speech over the past few weeks.

'The wedding is in two days' time—shouldn't you start?'

'I'll get around to it at some point. If I have to, I'll just wing it on the day.'

'You can't *wing it*!'

'Why not?'

'Are you kidding me? With *your* views on love and marriage, you might well say something totally inappropriate.' She paused and shook her head frantically, her hands flying upwards in disbelief. 'Like offering your condolences rather than congratulations. The best man's speech is too important—you can't just *wing it*.'

'Grace, I've presented to thousands at industry conferences worldwide, in a multitude of languages. I think I can handle a wedding speech.'

'Have you given one before?'

'Several times.'

She eyed him for a few seconds. 'Were they before your divorce?'

'What if they were?'

'Well, I'm guessing that your views might be very different now.'

He knew only too well that they were. 'Look, I'm busy now, but I'll pull something together later tonight or tomorrow.'

At that, Grace walked over to his desk and from behind her back brought forward a book, which she dropped onto a set of architectural drawings for a new office block in Melbourne.

He picked it up. She had to be joking. 'Are you being serious? *The Best Man's Survival Manual.*'

She gave him a triumphant smile. 'The wedding planner gave it to me. Apparently she always carries one for emergencies.'

He threw her a disparaging glance. 'The next time I meet with the team at the disaster recovery charity I sponsor, I'll have to check that they carry one at all times.'

She gave him an even brighter smile. 'Hah, very funny. Now, how about I help you pull it together?'

He gestured once again to his desk. 'I'm busy. And I have an urgent conference call in two hours I need to prepare for.'

'Twenty minutes—no more. I promise.'

'Grace, I have to warn you I'm on to you, I overheard your conversation with the wedding planner earlier. I know your technique. You're not going to wear me down by refusing to go away.'

'I'm not!'

She was, but now was not the time to get into that argument. He wanted to get back to his work. 'Why are you doing this?' he asked.

Her laughter died and she sat down on the seat opposite his desk. The indigo denim made her violet eyes

shine brighter than ever. 'You helped me with the flowers—I'd like to help you in return.'

'I don't need help.'

'Fine. Wing your speech for me now, and if it's up to
scratch then I'll leave you alone.'

He knew she wasn't going to leave without a fight—
and anyway he never had been able to resist a dare.

He flew through his introduction and then launched
into some witty anecdotes about Christos, one of which
even had Grace snorting with laughter. But then he dried
up. And died spectacularly. He didn't know what else to
say. How could he celebrate marriage and love when he
didn't believe in either?

He glanced at Grace and then away again—away from
the sympathy in her eyes.

'I shouldn't have agreed to be best man.'

'I think it's admirable that you did. It means the world
to Christos.'

Guilt churned inside him. He couldn't let Christos
down. But right now he wanted to forget the speech, in
fact forget the whole wedding.

With a raised eyebrow he deftly changed the subject.
'Christos rang earlier. Sofia and he are delighted we're
getting on so well.'

To that she gave a guilty smile. 'Sofia rang me last
night. What was I going to say? That you're against the
wedding...? That I'm way behind with the flowers? That
we disagree on just about everything?'

'Not everything. Apparently you think I'm hot.'

It took a few seconds for Grace to compute what Andreas
had just said. 'What? *No!* Oh, I'm going to kill Sofia
when she gets here. We were just messing around on the
phone... She kept asking me what I thought of you. I only

said it as a joke, to get her off my back. She's always trying to set me up with unsuitable guys.'

He sat back in his chair and folded his arms. 'So I'm unsuitable now?'

'Of course you are. You don't believe in love, commitment, marriage. Need I go on?'

'Hey, but I'm hot—what more do you need?'

Oh, this was excruciating—especially as part of her agreed with him. But if she was going to remain sane for the next few days she couldn't go there.

'It was a joke.' For a second she pressed the palm of her hand against the raging heat on her cheeks. Time to change the subject. 'Back to the speech. Twenty minutes and we'll pull it together. Are you on?'

He considered her for a while and she willed him not to move the conversation back to whether she thought he was hot or not. At first a grin played at the corners of his mouth, but then he cleared his throat, contemplated the messy pile of paper on his desk and shook his head wryly. 'You've been here ten minutes already—you have ten minutes left.'

'Fine. Okay, it was a great start, but now you need to praise Sofia and then finish on your hopes for them as a couple. Let's focus on the last point first: your hopes for them. What *do* you wish for them?'

'I don't know…to be happy-ever-after?'

'Too much of a cliché. Think harder.'

Andreas gave her an exasperated stare and stood up. He walked to the window overlooking the terrace and the Aegean beyond. He rolled his shoulders before he turned to her.

'I spent my lunchtime with my lawyer, agreeing to pay off my ex who's now claiming rights to this island.'

She fidgeted in her seat when his eyes bored into her.

'I could have fought her in the courts, but that would have stopped me giving Christos his wedding present: ownership of half of this island. So forgive me for being a little cynical about marriage. Right now I'm not in the mood to think of anything other than romantic clichés, even knowing that they are unrealistic and unobtainable and the preserve of dreamers.'

Bewildered by the sudden change in his mood, she stood and walked towards him. 'Is that a dig at me?'

Irritation fired in his eyes. 'No, but you can take it as one if you want.'

They stared at each other, angry and frustrated, breathing heavily…and then their anger turned from annoyance to a simmering heat, and the atmosphere in the room grew thick with want and desire.

He crossed the few steps that separated them and yanked her into his arms, muttering words she didn't understand. Her body collided with his and before she could react his mouth was on hers. A hand on the back of her neck held her prisoner, while the other wrapped tight around her waist. For a brief second she tried to pull away, but then she became lost in the heady sensation of his mouth on hers, the intoxicating sweep of his tongue, the pleasure of his hand caressing her back. She wrapped her arms about his neck, deepening the kiss, her body instinctively moving against his hardness.

But then he suddenly pulled away and stepped back, and she stood there, dazed, her lips bruised, her body aching.

He ran a hand through his hair, his jaw flexed tight. 'I'm sorry. That wasn't a good idea.'

No man should be able to kiss like that. Her thoughts

ran in several directions all at once, bringing little sense. Why had he kissed her? What must he be like in bed if his kisses were so scorching? Why? Why? *Why?*

'Are you still in love with your ex?'

'What?'

He glared at her as though it was the most insane question ever, but to her it was the only thing that made sense of his anger and cynical views.

'Is that why you were so upset about the divorce?'

'No, I'm not still in love with my ex. And I'm not upset about my divorce—I'm angry about it.'

'Why?'

'Because I was blind for much too long as to how incompatible my ex and I were.'

'Incompatible in what way?'

'My ex wanted very different things in life to me. She only pretended to want what I did in order to marry me. She was more attracted to what I had than who I was.'

'You mean she married you for your money?'

'Yes. And I was too foolish to see it. Within weeks she was refusing to live here on the island, to spend time with my family. Her social life in Athens was more important.'

'Did you love her when you got married?'

His jaw worked, and he inhaled a deep breath before meeting her eye. 'At the time I thought it was love, but I came to realise that I'd mistaken physical attraction and passion for love.'

'Oh.' Every square inch of her skin was scarlet at this point. She should leave. 'I'm sorry.'

'Don't be sorry. Just learn from it… Love and marriage can be hell on earth.'

'God, Andreas, don't for one second think that I don't know that. I spent my entire childhood witnessing my dad's toxic take on marriage. I know there are bad marriages. But I also know there are wonderful ones. Sofia's parents' marriage, my grandparents'... Now Christos and Sofia's. Marriages that are loving partnerships of trust and respect. Marriages that aren't about judgement and criticism.'

'How can you be so idealistic?'

'Because I believe in love—that the right man is out there for me.'

'Waiting to whisk you away.'

'Yes. And I don't care if you think it's idealistic. To me it's a very real dream. I want a life partner. I want love. I want a man who thinks I'm the coolest thing ever. And I'm not going to settle for anything else.'

She could see a hundred thoughts flickering in the depths of his eyes: puzzlement, incredulity, a hint of tenderness. But then he walked back to his desk, shaking his head. Once he had sat down, he checked his watch.

'Our twenty minutes is up.' The sternness in his voice was matched by the harsh expression on his face; the faint scar above his eyebrow was once again more visible as he frowned. A scar to match the toughness in his soul...

A toughness she would have to feign herself. 'So it is. If you want any further help let me know. And for what it's worth I think you should remember how you felt about love prior to your marriage and include that in your speech.'

When he gave a noncommittal shrug and turned his attention back to his computer screen, she inhaled a deep breath.

'The pre-wedding dinner tomorrow night in Athens...?' she asked.

'My helicopter will collect us at five.'

Grace left the room and walked back towards the

workshops, her heart thumping in her chest. That kiss…
That kiss had been wonderful and sexy…and it had
landed her in a whole heap of trouble.

CHAPTER FIVE

THE FOLLOWING DAY raucous noise spilt through the villa: shouts from the kitchen, the sound of hammering out on the terrace. Andreas sent a final few emails to his office in Athens and shut down his computer; there was little point in trying to get any work done in this mayhem. Anyway, he had worked until three in the morning, resolving the Cayman Islands issues—he needed a break... And, okay, he'd admit it to himself: he wanted to see Grace.

Outside, a crew were fixing lights on to the temporary stage that had been erected on the terrace the day before. He hadn't seen Grace all day, and knew he had no business going in search of her now. It was asking for trouble. But kissing her last night had been unbelievable. For the first time in ages he had lost himself totally in the physical joy of holding a woman, tasting her rather than mentally working out what it was she wanted from him.

He approached the workshops with an eagerness that confounded but exhilarated him. Inside, he felt his enthusiasm waver when two strangers stared back at him. When they finally found their voices one of the women told him that Grace was down on the jetty, helping with the unloading of more supplies. Frustration that she was not alone had him turning abruptly away.

Back outside, he spotted her—lost amongst the potted trees crowding the jetty, which now resembled a small forest. The delivery boat was out in the harbour, sailing back towards Naxos.

As he neared the jetty Grace came towards him unsteadily, carrying one of the potted trees. He went to take it from her but she drew back.

'It's fine—it's not as heavy as it looks; the planter is made from lightweight fibreglass.'

She kept on walking and he called to her. 'Where are you taking it?'

She stopped at the end of the jetty and dropped the white sugar-cube-shaped planter down. 'I want to place the planters and the storm lamps at intervals between here and the chapel.'

Andreas glanced back at the endless planters and storm lamps crowding the jetty. 'Have you any help?'

She rushed back down the jetty and picked up another planter. 'The other florists are finishing off the final prep work and will come and help in a little while.'

She was all business, and barely gave him a glance. He tried not to let it get to him.

'If you take care of the storm lamps, I'll position the planters,' he said.

For a moment she hesitated, as though she was about to refuse his offer, but then she gave a brief nod.

'Thank you.' Picking up the two nearest storm lanterns, she rushed off the jetty, saying, 'The planters were supposed to be delivered this morning but have only just arrived. The other florists have to leave by five as they have to prepare the flowers for another wedding on Naxos tomorrow.'

In silence they worked together: Grace dropping the

storm lamps ten metres apart and he placing the planters in between.

As they moved up onto the path, where it cut along the cliff towards the chapel, her silence and her habit of rushing away from him at every opportunity put him further and further on edge.

They walked back towards the jetty again and he could take no more. He called to her as she walked in front of him. 'Is everything okay?'

She kept on walking, but through the thin material of her pale pink tee shirt he saw her shoulders tense.

'If it's about last night, I apologise.'

She stopped abruptly and swung around to him. 'Apologise?'

'For kissing you. I didn't mean to upset you.'

'You didn't upset me, but it can't happen again.'

She said it with such certainty he was sorely tempted to take her in his arms and test her resolve. But she was right. They were playing with fire.

For the next trip back up the cliff-face Grace insisted on carrying a planter, as she was now way ahead with laying the lanterns. The other florists had joined them, and it had been agreed that he and Grace would carry the planters out as far as the chapel and work backwards from there.

Again silence fell between them. The planter balanced on her hip, she walked before him. He tried hard not to stare at how her cut-off faded denim shorts showed the perfection of her bottom.

He caught up with her when she stopped to move the planter from one hip to the other. Her eyes scanned along the coastline and then she briefly closed her eyes and lifted her face to the afternoon sun.

When she opened her eyes she said quietly, 'Why have

you decided to give Christos half the island? It's incredibly generous.'

'Not generous; just the right thing to do. My uncle should have left it to us both, but he was too stubborn.'

'What happened?'

He gestured for them to continue walking. For a while he didn't speak as an internal argument raged inside him.

Don't answer. You need to distance yourself from her.

But I want to explain. I want her to understand some of the mess that is my life. Why we will never share the same dreams for the future.

'When my grandfather died the family business was left to my father and this island to my uncle. My father has very traditional ideas and he believed that Kasas should also have been left to him as the eldest son. The two brothers fought and didn't speak for years. My father forbade us ever to speak to our uncle again; he wasn't pleased when I disobeyed him. Christos was about to follow my lead, but he gave in when my mother pleaded with him not to do so. For my loyalty, my uncle decided to leave the island to me.'

'But that wasn't fair on Christos.'

'I know. My uncle, usually calm and logical about everything, simply refused to listen to reason. He was a proud man, and in his eyes Christos had chosen my father over him; chosen to side with my father's greed.'

She shifted the planter back to her other hip before asking, 'And now? How do you get on with your father?'

He gave a chortle at the hint of caution in her voice. 'I take it that he left an impression on you when you met him at the engagement party?'

She shrugged uncertainly. 'He likes to speak his mind.'

That was the understatement of the year. His father was opinionated and brash on a good day. His father's angry words about the dishonour brought to the family name echoed in his mind. His grip on the planter tightened as anger and guilt swirled in his chest.

'It's not the easiest of relationships; we're very different. When I was younger I tried to work in the family business, but my father is almost impossible to work with. He'd refuse to delegate authority, question every decision and often reverse them. When all the issues blew up over the inheritance I left.'

'Do you ever regret that?'

'For the upset it caused my mother? Yes. But otherwise, no. I've succeeded on my own terms. Even if at times I've paid the price.'

Grace slowed her pace. 'What do you mean?'

The turmoil and self-doubt of the past few years came back to him in sharp relief. 'The global recession hit my company hard.'

'And succeeding on your own... Was that to prove to him just how capable you are? That you don't need him to be successful?'

'I guess we have that in common...'

She nodded, and for a moment their eyes connected.

'It's not easy, hating a person you love—is it?' he asked.

She came to a stop and readjusted the planter in her hands. At first she frowned, but then she gave a small exhalation of breath. 'I never thought of it like that; but that's exactly how I feel. There's so much I hate about my father's behaviour, but deep down a part of me—reluctant as it is—loves him. I don't understand it, and it would be so much easier if I didn't... Love is such a strange thing, isn't it?'

'Strange, dangerous and unpredictable.'

Her lips pursed and she shook her head crossly. 'Sometimes, but for most it's the one true wonder of being alive.'

Aman! Had she no sense? 'Still dreaming of your prince and happy-ever-after?'

A storm brewed in her violet eyes and her lips drew into a firm line. She glared at him. 'Yes—and when he comes along I'll send you a postcard.'

With that she flounced away and he followed, amusement tugging at his lips even while he tried to ignore the jealousy curling in his stomach at the thought of her with another man.

The chapel was close now, but the planter was starting to weigh heavily in his arms. In a few long strides he caught up with her. 'Do you want to stop for a break?'

Despite the sheen of perspiration on her skin, she shook her head defiantly. 'No.'

'You're persistent, aren't you?'

She stared at him belligerently. 'You sound surprised. Why wouldn't I be?'

He gave a light shrug. 'Most of the women I know aren't too keen on hard physical work.'

'From what I hear, you don't hang around long enough to find out. Maybe those women have a lot more going for them than you give them credit for.' With that she stalked away, and dropped the first planter at the bottom of the chapel terrace.

He dumped his ten metres away. 'So what do you suggest? That I stay and give them all hope of a relationship?'

'No, because you're obviously incapable of having one. I don't want any women getting hurt. But maybe you shouldn't make assumptions about them.'

How sheltered a life had she lived? She'd obviously had the good fortune never to encounter the sycophants he had. 'Are you *really* that innocent, Grace?'

Those violet eyes flared with anger. 'You know what, Andreas? Maybe I am. But I prefer to see the good in human nature.'

Those photographs he had been sent two years ago had shown him the truth about human nature.

With a bitter taste in his mouth, he answered, 'And *that's* where we will always differ.'

Why had someone so beautiful on the outside but so cynical at heart been sent into her life? The gods were truly having a laugh at her expense.

Grace twisted away from him, her blood boiling. She was tired and hungry, stressed about tomorrow, and plagued with an attraction to the six-foot-two, dark and sexy sceptic walking behind her.

If only it was that straightforward.

Though she hated to admit it, and even though Andreas was so disparaging about love and the motives of women, at his core he was a good man. He'd shown care towards her on numerous occasions; he clearly loved his family despite the differences between him and his father. It was as if he wore his scepticism as an armour.

But she had meant it when she'd said that she would never try to change a man. She wanted a man to fall in love with her with no games involved—no persuasion, no pretending she was something she wasn't. More than anything she wanted a relationship based on honesty and respect.

Her phone rang in her pocket and, pulling it out, she answered Matt's call, glad to have a distraction from the pain lancing through at the memory that her mum hadn't even bothered to leave a note when she had walked out on them.

Though Matt professed that nothing was wrong, and

that he'd just called to say hi, she immediately knew he was upset. With Matt she always had to draw him out gradually. They were back at the chapel with the next set of planters when she finally hung up on the call.

She dropped her planter onto the path and was about to pass Andreas when he placed a hand on her arm.

His eyes soft and concerned, he stepped closer. His hand moved up to lie gently on her upper arm. 'Are you okay? You seem tired?'

She wanted to say no, she wasn't okay. That she wanted him to hold her. To tell her everything would be okay. That Matt and Lizzie would do well in life. That tomorrow was going to be okay.

Instead she glanced at the time on her phone and then towards the jetty and the remaining planters. 'I'm not going to be able to go to the pre-wedding reception tonight... I still have so much to do.'

'Ioannis will be back from Naxos soon. He can take over the positioning of the planters.'

'It's not just the planters. I have a lot of other prep work that needs to be completed. Sofia is arriving here at eleven tomorrow, and I want to spend time with her. I need to have all the flowers ready in the workshop by then, for the local florists to position just before the ceremony begins.'

'I'll stay and help.'

'No! Absolutely not.'

But before she knew what was happening Andreas was on his phone. He spoke in Greek, but she understood his greeting to Christos.

Wearing denim jeans and a white polo shirt, now smeared with earth from the planters, he stood watching her as he spoke, his dark hair glistening under the sun, his voice a low and rapid flow of passionate sounds incomprehensible to her.

Her insides melted as his eyes roamed up and down her body. Something dark and dangerous was building in them as the call continued.

When he'd hung up, he gestured for them to start walking again. 'I spoke to Christos and explained that you were tied up with preparations. He told Sofia and she asked him to send her love. They both insisted that I should stay and help. And they agreed that I should take you out to dinner later.'

'They did not!'

'Call them if you don't believe me.'

He was calling her bluff. Well, she'd show him. 'Fine— I will.'

A few minutes later she hung up on her call to Sofia. Though disappointed that Grace would miss tonight, Sofia had been more concerned that Grace was putting herself under too much pressure. And, though Sofia had tried her best to disguise it, Grace had heard the fear in her voice that the flowers mightn't be ready for tomorrow.

After spending an age reassuring Sofia that she had everything under control, Grace hadn't even bothered to get into an argument about Andreas staying on with her.

'Apparently dinner was your idea?'

He didn't even have the decency to look abashed. 'You can't visit the Cyclades and not see some of the other islands.'

Dinner was *so* not going to happen. 'I won't be finished until very late.'

'How late?'

She deliberately adopted a look of grave consideration. 'Oh, at least eleven.'

He gave a smile that was much too smug for her liking.

'That's not a problem—we eat late here in Greece.' With that Andreas picked up his phone again and spoke briefly in Greek.

When they got back to the jetty, he steered her away and back towards the villa.

She gestured to the pots still on the jetty. 'We need to finish the planters.'

'You need a break first.'

He led her down onto one of the lower terraces built into the cliff-face, where a tray of food was awaiting them on a rattan dining table. Despite herself, Grace sank down onto the plump cream cushions of a rattan chair with a sigh, welcoming the shade provided by the raised parasol at the centre of the table.

Andreas poured some homemade lemonade for them both and uncovered a basket of bread and a selection of dips. Another basket held a selection of freshly baked pastries.

Grace greedily gulped the lemonade, only now realising just how thirsty she was.

'Why do you push yourself so hard?'

She lowered her glass to the table. 'I don't think I do...but I grew up with my dad's exacting standards. I suppose I'm still trying to meet those in some way. But, also, I want to deliver the best service that I can. I take my commitments and responsibilities very seriously.'

Andreas leaned forward and broke a bread roll in two. He handed a piece to her. 'Including your responsibilities to your brother and sister?'

'Yes.'

He regarded her thoughtfully. 'Why?'

She busied herself with breaking her roll into smaller pieces. 'When my mum left they had no one else. They were children. They needed someone to care for them.'

'How did it affect them?'

'Matt went quiet and barely spoke for a year…'

Grace stopped for a moment as memories caused her throat to thicken painfully. An unaccountable emotional force shifted around in her chest, as though it was searching for a way out. And suddenly she needed to tell him it all, so that he would understand why her heart had broken every single day in the year after her mum left.

'He used to get up early every morning…' She met Andreas's eye and then gazed away. 'He'd get up to wash his sheets. I used to have to pretend that I didn't notice the load in the tumble drier. I thought Lizzie was coping—she seemed her usual bubbly self—but then one day I was cleaning her bedroom and found that she was hoarding food…which accounted for her clothes not fitting any longer.'

'I'm sorry.'

She forced herself to shrug. 'It was tough, but now we're really close because of having gone through it together—so I guess some good has come from it all.'

'Do you miss them?'

Unexpected tears sprang to her eyes at his question and, perplexed by their suddenness and the powerful loneliness rolling through her, she took a while before she managed to speak. 'I miss them terribly. I miss our little family. I miss being loved.'

'They still love you.'

The gaping hole inside her widened at his words. How would he react if she told him just how desperate she was to be in love? To find companionship and security, fun and exhilaration?

'I know…but it's not the same when we're apart. And Lizzie's dating now. They're both moving on.'

'Do you ever see your mum now?'

Her heart lurched at his question. 'No. At first I was mad as hell with her and refused to, but after a while I came to understand why she'd left… After years of putting up with my father, it was kind of understandable. But by then we had drifted apart from her—to have got back in contact would have been like opening an old wound.' She gave him a wobbly smile and stood. 'Anyway, we don't have time for this now. I'd better get back to work.'

Andreas stood and walked towards her. Next thing she knew she was in his arms, being given the biggest bear hug of her life. His arms wrapped around her and he lowered his chin onto the top of her head. His arm blocked her eyes so that she was in a cocoon of darkness. She inhaled his scent, a mixture of lemon and fresh salty perspiration, so earthy and male she felt dizzy with the desire to lift his tee shirt and press her nose against his damp skin.

For a moment every worry, every painful memory disappeared as she was held in his protective embrace. Her rigid body slowly melted against him and she gave a little sigh. He drew back and smiled down at her.

Dazed, she hoped her eyes weren't rolling in her head. 'You give a very good hug.'

His thumb ran the length of her cheek. 'I'm here any time you need one.'

For a moment they both smiled at each other, but then she pulled away. She was in serious danger of feeling things she could not afford to for a man intent on never having love in his life.

As they walked back to the workshops Andreas wondered what was happening to him. He didn't hold women like that, want to protect them, wipe out every painful memory for them.

Beside him, Grace gave a contented sigh. 'I haven't travelled to many countries, but Kasas Island has to be the most beautiful place in the world.'

Something dormant in him stirred at her words. When had he stopped enjoying this island? Stopped taking the time to relax in its simple pleasures? For the past two years he had driven himself relentlessly at work, and the island had become a refuge rather than a place he truly enjoyed.

But then a warning bell sounded in his brain. How often had his ex claimed the same?

'You'd tire of it once the novelty wore off.'

She stopped dead and stared at him. 'No, I wouldn't.' She cocked her head to the side. 'You don't believe me, do you?'

Why was he standing here arguing with her? He started to walk away. 'It doesn't matter.'

She caught up with him and pulled him to a stop. 'It might not matter to you, but I'm fed up with the fact that you don't trust me, Andreas. You constantly pull back from telling me about yourself. You'll go so far and then the shutters go down as though you don't trust me. You look at me as though you don't believe what I say. What have I done that makes you think I'm untrustworthy?'

'Come on, Grace, I barely know you.'

'You know me well enough to kiss me senseless.'

She stared at him so indignantly he could not help but smile. 'I kissed you *senseless*?'

Her eyes narrowed and she stamped a foot on the path. 'Wrong phrase—ignore it. Now, are you going to answer my question?'

He took a step closer, his shadow falling over her. He lowered his head and inhaled her scent, his voice automatically turning into a low baritone. 'I have a question for you first: can I kiss you?'

Her violet eyes shadowed and her cheeks flushed deeply. 'I... Not until you promise me that you're going to start trusting me. That you don't think I'm lying to you or that I want anything from you.'

'You drive a hard bargain.'

'You have to mean it. I'm trusting you not to pretend, not to lie to me.'

He drew back, paralysed with indecision. Could he honestly tell her that he trusted her? His stomach was a knot, his heart a time bomb ready to explode. Others might lie, but that was anathema to him. He could just walk away now—go back to the way his life had been a few short days ago. But, gazing deep into her eyes, he realised that he didn't want to this to end—not yet—and that he believed he *could* trust her.

'I trust you.'

She gave him a solemn smile, and when he ran his hand along her cheek she leaned into it.

And then he walked away.

CHAPTER SIX

GRACE STOOD ON the path, dumbstruck. What had happened to their kiss?

She chased after him. 'Did I just miss something?'

He stopped by the steps up to the workshops, his expression sombre. 'You said you wanted to trust in me. Which means that you'll trust me to look out for you, not to hurt you. With that being the case, there's no way that I can kiss you—because, frankly, I don't know where it could lead.'

He was right. Of course he was. She just wished she didn't feel so upset at the prospect of all this being over so quickly. That their kiss last night had been the end of the line for them.

'My helicopter will be here to collect us at eleven. I'll help Ioannis with the remaining planters. What else can we do to help you?'

His businesslike attitude pulled her up short. She needed to start focusing on the wedding.

'The candles need to be placed inside the lanterns...' She paused and gave him a pleading smile. 'And two white ribbons need to be tied to each of the bay trees.'

He inhaled a deep breath. 'If you *dare* tell Christos that I was tying ribbons you'll be in big trouble.'

He looked so hacked off she couldn't help but giggle. And once she started she couldn't stop, because he was studying her so incredulously. But eventually he too laughed, his laughter coming from deep inside him was highly infectious, which only caused Grace to start her 'hiccupping hyena' impression, as Sofia so charmingly called it. He stopped and stared at her, clearly surprised, but then he laughed even harder.

When their laughter eventually petered out he shook his head and eyed her with amusement. 'You do crazy things to me, Grace Chapman.'

With that he walked away, and she stared after him, knowing, despite their differences, that she had never felt so in tune with another person in all her life.

Later that night Grace ran towards the villa. She had fifteen minutes to get ready. Not enough time to wash her hair. *Just great.* She was going out for dinner with the sexiest man she had ever met with unwashed hair and make-up slapped on. But then maybe it was for the best. Maybe he would take one look at her and the attraction between them would wilt.

She took a quick shower and whilst dragging a towel over her body in order to dry herself hopped from one foot to the other in front of the wardrobe, trying to decide what to wear. Would the cocktail dress she had bought especially for the pre-wedding reception tonight be too over the top? Send the wrong message? But all her other clothes were too casual.

She yanked the dress from the wardrobe and pulled it on. Five minutes to go. Quickly she applied some foundation and cream eyeshadow, a rose-pink gloss on her lips. She tied her hair back into a ponytail. A quick spritz of perfume and she was out through the door.

Andreas was waiting for her by the patio doors in the living room, staring out onto the terrace.

She came to an abrupt stop beside him. 'Ready?'

He stood back and his eyes trailed slowly down over her body. He cleared his throat before he spoke. 'You look incredible.'

All evening she had firmly reminded herself that to get involved with Andreas would be a major mistake. Past experience had taught her the awful pain of having someone walk away from her—which undoubtedly *would* happen should she get entangled with this oh-so-gorgeous playboy. This was just a cordial dinner between...

Between what? She had no idea how to define their relationship, but maybe 'friends' was the most suitable description. But how was she supposed to deal with the heat in his eyes and the pull of desire coiling within her?

She gave him a quick smile. 'Thank you...and you don't look half bad yourself.' Which was the understatement of the year. He was freshly showered, and his damp hair was tamer than usual, which emphasised the impossible height of his cheekbones, the green brilliance of his eyes. His dark navy suit fitted him to perfection, the snow-white shirt open at the neck highlighting the golden tones of his skin. She would never get to touch him, to trace her fingers over his skin, to feel the hard muscle underneath...

'Why are you carrying your sandals?'

She tore her eyes away from him and dangled her stiletto heels to swing between them. 'There's no way I'll climb the hill to the helicopter wearing *these* bad boys.'

His gaze travelled downwards and her French polished toes curled when his gaze remained at her feet. When he eventually looked back up there was a new tension to his jaw.

'Your feet will get dirty. Put them on and you can hold my arm—I'll help you to the helicopter.'

Grace sat on the side of a sofa and bent over to place her feet in the sandals. The sandals were new, and she struggled to fasten the strap, the metal bar refusing to go into the tiny eyelet pierced in the dark navy leather strap. She gritted her teeth and pushed as hard as she could, while her hip bone screamed at the awkward position she was leaning over in.

'Sit back and I'll try.'

Before she had time to protest Andreas was crouched down before her. He gently lifted her foot and balanced it on his thigh. She bit down on the dual temptations fighting within her: to pull away—his touch was way too much for a woman already on a knife-edge of temptation—or sigh so loudly she would be heard over on Naxos.

When he was done, he stood up and held his hand out to her. For a moment she hesitated. More than ever this evening seemed like a thoroughly bad idea.

As though reading her mind, Andreas said, 'We're going out for dinner and a little fun—nothing serious.'

Three days ago she had closed the door to her minuscule apartment in Bristol, full of dreams for the future, hoping for excitement. Well, boy, had she got it—in a bucket full. And although she knew she was dancing with danger maybe, just for tonight, she could embrace this crazy scenario and relish being in the company of this utterly gorgeous man.

He was going to have a heart attack. Grace's dress was too much. A mid-thigh-length navy lace wrap dress, embellished with sequins, it was far too short and far too figure-hugging. Way too much flesh was revealed in the deep scoop that ended at the tip of the valley between her breasts. And what was *really* driving his pulse berserk was the knowledge that with a simple tug of the satin ribbon sitting at her waist it would come undone.

How was he supposed to act like a gentleman tonight when she was wearing that?

Next to him in the helicopter, she folded one leg over the other, and he groaned inwardly at the sight of her toned thighs. Thin straps of dark navy leather criss-crossed her foot, which dangled provocatively in front of him, and a jolt of unwanted desire barged through him. Earlier, as he had buckled her sandal, his fingers had trailed against the smooth skin of her slender ankle and he'd had to battle hard against the urge to keep trailing his fingers upwards.

Her words this afternoon that she wanted to trust in him came back to taunt him. He couldn't abuse that trust. He couldn't seduce her as he so desperately wanted to do. Grace believed in love and romance, in happy-ever-after; he had to respect everything she wanted even if the tension of attraction and desire between them was so thick right now he could almost punch it. He had to keep this light and fun—keep the conversation neutral.

'Did you finish all the prep work?'

She gave him a bright grin of relief. 'Yes. All the major displays are finished. I just have to complete the bouquets in the morning.' She puffed out her cheeks. 'I can't believe Sofia's getting married tomorrow; it's all happened so quickly. I need to start getting my head around my chief bridesmaid's duties. Talking of which—have you completed your speech?'

He shifted in his seat. 'Almost.'

She gave him a knowing look. 'Can I help in any way?'

He didn't want to talk about the speech—his ongoing nemesis for reasons he didn't fully understand. 'No, I plan on finishing it tomorrow morning. Christos and my parents aren't arriving until lunchtime.'

For a moment she paused and worried at her lip, doubt clouding her eyes. 'How do you feel about the wedding now?'

Ambivalent was the word that best summed up how he felt about tomorrow…and it was something he didn't want to overthink. Right now he just wanted to pretend it wasn't happening.

'If you're worried that I might object to the vows, or share my views on relationships in my speech, don't worry. I promise to be the perfect best man tomorrow.'

At first she beamed with relief, but then her face clouded with tension. She glanced at him, and then away, and then her eyes darted back to him. 'Do you think the flowers will be okay?'

The fear in her eyes was so sudden and intense his heart jolted. He twisted fully in his seat and placed a hand on hers. 'Grace, I know nothing about flowers. I've been to endless weddings, even my own, and didn't notice them. But even I can see how spectacular yours are. After tomorrow you'll be turning away bookings.'

Her eyes shone with gratitude. 'Thank you.'

The helicopter began to hover down towards the restaurant, which sat high on a clifftop on Santorini Island. Once it had landed Andreas helped Grace out, and as they neared the building the heavy beat of music greeted them.

Friday night was party night at the Ice Cocktail Bar and Restaurant.

He had to lean low, so that Grace could hear him above the music. 'How about we get a cocktail to start and then eat?'

The bar was busy, and as usual the central floor space

had become a dance floor. The music was a fast constant beat, energetic and sensual.

He glanced down when Grace's hand touched against his arm. She reached up to shout in his ear.

'This bar is amazing... I've never seen so many people enjoying themselves so much.'

Her breath tickled his ear. Desire gripped him hard and he had the sudden urge to turn around and lead her somewhere quiet. He bit down on the temptation and taking her hand in his, led her through the throng.

As usual his friend Georgios, Ice's owner, was sitting in the far corner. When Georgios saw him approach he jumped up and the two men embraced. After Andreas had introduced Grace, Georgios insisted they take his seats and promised to return with two of the house specials.

They attempted to have a conversation, but the music was too loud, so they sat sipping their gin and ginger cocktails, watching the dancers out on the dance floor, their movement so carefree and joyful it was addictive. His heartbeat pounded in time with the music, and when Grace moved beside him, her thigh grazing against his, he turned to her.

Her eyes were bright, her skin flushed, and she leaned towards him, a slow smile breaking on her lips. 'Do you want to dance?'

Sense and caution went out of the window at her question, which had been asked in a low voice, whispered against his ear.

He stood and removed his jacket and led her out on to the dance floor, pulling her into the centre of the action.

Her arms reached upwards and her body swayed to the music, her head thrown back. Strobe lights flashed over her tilted face, highlighting the plumpness of her glossy lips, the sultry look in her eyes. The light danced on the sequins of her sexy dress, and the thought of pulling that ribbon and revealing what lay beneath sent firecrackers of desire through his system.

For a few seconds he watched her, trying to resist the inevitable, but then he reached out and pulled her towards him, his hands on her waist, and together their bodies dipped and swayed, their eyes never leaving one another.

Lithe, and with perfect timing, Andreas held her to him, his body lightly controlling her movements. She was on fire. It was all wrong. But right now she didn't care. It felt too good. She felt alive and young and carefree.

Through his shirt her fingers touched against the taut bulk of his biceps. His hips moved against hers and an ache grew in her belly. His hand moved up from her waist and for a brief moment his thumb ran along the side of her breast. She gave him a brief smile and he smiled back, his eyes darkening.

The ache in her belly spread outwards and her breasts grew tight and sensitive. The hard muscles of his thighs pushed against hers, and then he shifted her so that one of her legs was in between his. The ache spread even further, until all her insides felt hollow.

His hands moved around to her back. One held her at the waist while the other splayed downwards, touching the sensitive point at the bottom of her spine. She arched even further into him, her breath catching as his hip bone pushed against her.

She stared at the smooth line of his freshly shaved jaw, fighting the desire to trace her lips against the warm skin. His hard body and his scent of lemons with an undertone of spice tugged her under, into a world where no one but he existed.

Much too quickly the music came to an end. For a brief moment his lips swooped down and he planted a hot kiss on her exposed collarbone. He led her off the dance floor, dazed, and she was unable to wipe the grin from her mouth.

When they reached their seats she sat down, but Andreas remained standing. He took his phone from his back trouser pocket and his brow furrowed when he checked the screen. He pointed at it, and then out to the outside terrace. She nodded and waved towards him, telling him that it was okay for him to go and make a call.

When he was gone an involuntary shiver ran through her body. She was definitely dancing with danger. And she didn't know if she was going to be able to stop.

Andreas sat at a table out on the terrace to return his missed call from Christos. Unlike the other customers, who were all facing outwards towards the spectacle of the night sky, he faced back into the bar, where he had the perfect view of Grace, sitting in front of a low window.

His fear that something was wrong was immediately put to rest when Christos assured him that he was just calling to check that everything was in place for tomorrow. With a jolt Andreas realised that his usually laid-back brother was nervous—*very* nervous, in fact. Guilt pricked against his skin. Yes, he had fulfilled his best man duties so far—including organising a bachelor party last week in Athens—but had he really been there for Christos?

When he thought of the calls Grace shared with Matt and Lizzie, full of warmth and genuine concern and interest, he realised how amiss he had been—both recently and in the past few years. Three days ago he had had no idea that the hopeless romantic he had rescued at the airport would cause him to pause and take stock of his own life.

He deliberately went through a detailed breakdown with Christos, of everything the planner and Grace had done for tomorrow, and then ran through the itinerary for the day again. But as he spoke he got increasingly distracted. A man had approached Grace. He sat down beside her—much too close for Andreas's liking. What was he playing at? And why the hell was she smiling back at him, being so friendly?

Jealous fire raged through his veins. But then Grace turned around and pointed at him. The other man gave him an uncertain smile and backed off. Unbelievably, twice more this happened during the course of his conversation with Christos, before he was able to end the call.

Grace smiled up in relief when Andreas returned. The call had been much longer than she'd expected and she was hungry...for food *and* his company.

His earlier ease was gone, though. His expression was tense, and his eyes barely reached hers.

'Our table is ready in the restaurant.'

She followed him out on to the terrace and then down stone steps to a lower level terrace. Their table was next to a glass balustrade which gave unending views out on to the Aegean and to the lights of the towns to the west. The whole terrace was awash with candles on white tabletops and storm lanterns on the white concrete floors.

Andreas recommended the house special, lobster spaghetti, which they both ordered—along with a bottle of the local *assyrtiko* white wine.

Throughout the ordering process Andreas seemed distracted, and once their waiter had left she asked, 'Is everything okay?'

'Do you usually get so much attention when you're out?'

Perplexed, she sat back into the cushions of her chair. 'What do you mean?'

'When I was on my call several men approached you.'

'So?'

Cold eyes challenged hers. 'Why?'

She recoiled for a moment, at the cynicism in his voice, but then she sat forward and challenged him back. 'Why did they approach me? Oh, come on, Andreas, why are you asking me that? We both know why... They wanted to buy me a drink but I said no, that I was waiting for you.'

He made no response, but kept on staring at her sceptically.

Anger and disappointment collided within her and she said bitterly, 'A few hours ago you said you trusted me. Were you lying?'

He still said nothing, and she knew this night was over.

She placed her napkin on her plate. 'I don't feel hungry any longer. I want to go back to Kasas.'

She went to move, but his hand snapped around her wrist. His eyes were furious, but also shadowed with confusion.

'Why did you refuse their drinks...? It's not as if we are a couple.'

She jerked back in shock. 'Are you angry that I refused? Did you want me to accept?'

He shook his head vigorously. 'Of course not... But there was nothing stopping you, so why didn't you?'

Totally bewildered, she answered, 'Because I'm with *you*. Yes, we might not be a couple, but we *are* out together...why would I accept a drink from another man?'

'To play mind games with me—to make me jealous.'

Frustration surged through her. 'Good·God, what do you take me for? I'm not that type of person. I don't play games. I don't hurt other people.'

For a while he stared at her, his jaw flexing. His mouth became a tight grimace. 'I'm sorry. That was uncalled for.'

His remorse looked genuine, but he had some explaining to do and she wasn't going to let him off the hook. 'If you're sorry, prove it to me. Explain what the last fifteen minutes has been about.'

A waiter arrived with their food, but Andreas spoke to him in Greek and the waiter walked away with the plates.

'I told him we weren't ready and that we'd order again when we are.'

She nodded and waited for him to speak.

His hand rubbed against his cheek and then ran up into his hair, messing it up just the way she loved. Oh, why was she so attracted to this man who had *heartbreaker* written all over him?

Andreas felt sick to his stomach. He had behaved abominably. Grace deserved an explanation. But the thought of recounting the past was tearing him apart. His sense of self, his certainty of who he was, felt as unstable as the flickering flames on the candles at the centre of their table.

'Two years ago I received a blackmail threat. A member of the paparazzi had photos of my wife making love to another man on his yacht.'

Grace's hand moved towards his but he pulled away. He didn't want her pity. They sat in silence and eventually he gazed towards her. There wasn't pity in her eyes, but anger. He frowned, and she answered his unspoken question.

'I hope you reported him to the police and told *her* exactly what you thought of her. How could she have done that to you?'

Thrown by her outraged disbelief, he paused, unable to find an answer. Her outrage almost made him want to smile. Grace was a fierce protector; no wonder she'd taken on the task of protecting her siblings.

'How could I have married her, more like.' The exact question his father had shouted at him, accusing him of bringing dishonour into the family.

'What happened between you, Andreas...? Why did she do something so awful?'

'When I confronted her she said she was lonely, that she hated living on Kasas, and the amount of travel I did.'

'It doesn't sound like you believed her.'

'I was away because the recession had taken hold.' Inhaling a deep breath, he arched his neck back and stared briefly up into the night sky; the stars seemed impossibly far away. 'My businesses were struggling in the worldwide property crash, but I knew that, even though it was high risk, it was my opportunity to radically extend my asset base—which would firmly secure the future of the company. I travelled the world, persuading investment firms to finance my property deals. Unfortunately my ex did not agree with my expansion plans, nor the risks involved—and nor the way it curtailed our cash flow. So she had an affair with a man who could provide her with the lifestyle she had expected when we married—a man I had considered a friend.'

Grace considered him nervously and shuffled in her seat before saying, 'You're a shrewd guy...'

'So why didn't I know what she was like when we

married? Because I believed her flattery.' His throat burning, he paused and then admitted, 'I trusted her at a time when I was trying to deal with my uncle's death and the fight with my father that was causing me to lose my family.'

'And you thought *she* could be your new family?'

She spoke so softly and with such emotion he felt the humiliation that had carried him through the conversation to this point evaporate. Only regret remained. 'Yes.'

'And your friend?'

A bitter taste grew in his mouth. 'He knows to stay out of my way.'

Her eyes trailed above his left eyebrow. 'That scar...'

'He came off much worse.'

The flicker of a grimace crossed her face for a moment. 'I'm sorry, Andreas. I'm sorry she caused you so much pain. Your friend too. I can't think of anything worse than being betrayed like that.'

'It taught me a valuable lesson: that I can never again believe I truly know another person.'

She moved forward, passion burning in her eyes. 'No, I don't agree. The timing of your marriage was terrible— you were grieving for your uncle. I think in normal circumstances most of us *can* know another person, even if it's just a gut instinct about them.'

'People wear masks—they tell you what they think you want to hear.'

'Let's put it to the test. How about me? Do you think I would cheat on a partner? On my husband?'

'How would I know?'

'Would I cheat, Andreas? Yes or no?'

Every fibre of his body knew that she wouldn't. But it was hard to admit that his long-held views were wrong—

that in a few short days this woman had turned so many of them upside down.

He inhaled a deep breath and said tersely, 'No.'

'You're right. I wouldn't. Because when I marry it will be for love and because I respect my husband. I want a hundred per cent honesty and trust in a relationship. I will never lie, never play games... My marriage will be too important to me to ever even contemplate compromising it.'

'Your husband will be a very lucky man.'

She gave him a rueful smile. 'I just need to meet him.'

Something hard kicked inside him at the thought of her married to another man. His mind jumped ahead to her leaving Kasas, leaving *him*. 'When are you leaving?'

She tapped a fingernail on the bottom of her fork before she gazed up with a sad smile. 'Monday.'

'Two more days.'

Her smile faded.

His heart began to pound. Could he let her go? Could a brief passionate kiss be all that they ever shared?

CHAPTER SEVEN

LATER THAT NIGHT, back on Kasas, Grace's heart did a funny little jump of delight when Andreas held her hand all the way from the helipad down to the villa.

When they entered the living room, the silence that had been with them for the entire journey home from Santorini continued to bounce between them. It was a silence born from the intensity of the connection they had shared tonight—a connection of emotional honesty.

Andreas opening up about his marriage had changed everything. He had let her into his world, trusted her. He had reached out to her. And she wasn't sure what to do with the emotional chasm that sat in her heart as a result. A chasm full of hunger to connect with him even further. To know him to the depths of his very being. A hunger to express her feelings towards him.

The chasm had her wanting to reach out to him, but she didn't know how. She was scared she would do the wrong thing. Her old self-doubts sat like a cloak on her shoulders.

'Would you like a drink?'

Uncertainty had her dithering for an embarrassing few seconds before she said, 'I think I should go to bed. It's almost two and I have to be up early. Thank you for a lovely night.'

His eyes searched hers for a moment before he nodded. But as she turned away he said, 'Wait. I have something I want to give to you.'

He disappeared upstairs and, intrigued, Grace waited on the edge of the sofa where he had earlier fastened her sandals, a shiver running through her body when she remembered the tender touch of his hands on her ankle.

When he returned, he reached out and said, 'Give me your hand and close your eyes.'

'What are you up to?'

'Just close your eyes. You'll see in a few minutes.'

Grace held out her hand cautiously, and it was just as well that he had told her to close her eyes as she did so anyway, involuntarily, when his fingers held her hand. His thumb stroked down the sensitive skin of her inner wrist. Goosebumps ran the length of her body.

In a low voice that had her jerking forward with a need to close the distance between them he said, 'I was going to give this to you tomorrow, but...'

'But what?'

'We'll probably both be too busy.'

His fingernails lightly grazed against her skin and she giggled. 'That tickles. What *are* you doing?'

'Sit still. You wriggling like that isn't helping.'

Grace inhaled a deep breath and tried to ignore his fingertips stroking her wrist, the way that simple touch was setting her alight, making her yearn for more.

And then her body stilled, although her heart exploded in her chest as a sudden realisation hit home: the empty ache of loneliness that had been her constant companion for so many years was gone. With Andreas she felt whole, somehow. Safe and protected. Understood.

Panic flared inside her. She needed to see him. *Now.* 'I want to open my eyes.'

'In a few seconds.'

His fingers continued to dance on her wrist and she had to squeeze her eyes to stop the burning temptation to fling them open and drink him in. They had so little time left together.

'Now open them.'

On her silver bracelet sat a new charm—an intricate violet flower, its purple-blue design sitting between the miniature flower clippers and the violin that Matt and Lizzie had given her last Christmas. She wore the bracelet as a constant reminder of them; it felt right that Andreas's charm sat with theirs.

She ran a fingertip over the exquisite design. 'It's so pretty...thank you. Why a violet?'

He gazed down at the charm. 'Because it symbolises courage and intelligence.'

She couldn't stifle her giggle. 'You just made that up! And anyway, it symbolises modesty.'

His brows knitted together in consternation. 'Does it?' He gave her a sheepish look. 'I definitely didn't buy it for that reason.'

His expression grew serious and he leaned over to touch the flower charm, his finger briefly brushing against her skin, sending every nerve-ending into a tailspin of desire.

'I bought it to thank you on behalf of my family for everything you've done to make tomorrow special.' His fingers stilled on her wrist. His voice grew deeper. 'And because it's the same incredible colour as your eyes.'

She stood up, her body shaking with the intensity of the emotions surging through her. It couldn't end like this. She couldn't walk away from him without being true to herself.

Her heart raced even faster, and though her stomach

churned she forced herself to speak. 'Stay with me to-night.'

Shock replaced the earlier heat in his eyes. 'What?'

Had she misread this whole situation? But she had seen how he had stared at her all night, felt how he had held her in the bar when they danced.

A deep blush flashed on her cheeks and she went to leave.

He stood in her way. 'Hold on—where are you going?'

She shook her head but kept it dipped down, too mortified to look him in the eye.

'You can't ask a man to stay the night and then run away before he even has the opportunity to reply.'

Humiliation had her answering sharply, 'Your expression was enough of an answer.'

'*Aman*, Grace! The sweetest, sexiest woman I have ever encountered has just asked me to stay the night... and we both know that I should say no.'

He thought she was sweet and sexy... But he was saying no. So she was lacking somehow. Was it the gulf between them career and wealth-wise? Their different backgrounds? Or was it that she simply wasn't attractive enough?

Hurt and humiliation twisted in her chest. 'Let's just forget this conversation ever happened.'

He ran a hand through his hair and a groan came from somewhere deep within him. 'Trust me—I would like nothing more than to spend the night with you. But I can't. I'm not what you're looking for, Grace.'

'Not in the long term, no...'

'You're playing with fire.'

She shook her head vigorously. She knew what she was doing. She had never been more certain of anything in all of her life.

'No, for the first time in many years I'm listening to what I really want.'

She paused, wishing she was brave enough to say everything that needed to be said. That she wanted fun and passion. Wanted to feel as physically close to him as she did emotionally. She searched for words, but everything seemed either too brash or needy.

And before she was able to find the right words Andreas stepped aside, his expression sombre.

'*Kalinichta*...goodnight, Grace.'

Grace's footsteps disappeared along the upstairs corridor and Andreas sank onto the sofa, tiredly dragging his hands over his face.

Turning Grace down had been one of the hardest things he had ever done.

What had he even been *thinking*? A gorgeous woman had invited him into her bed and he had said no!

But there were so many compelling reasons for doing so. The future they would share as part of Christos and Sofia's lives. The future Grace wanted. Her tender, soft heart. So many logical and reasonable arguments for staying the hell away from her.

Why, then, was he sitting here with regret storming through his veins, angry at the recognition that the past two years he had been living a lie, pretending he was content in his life?

Three short days with Grace had shown him just how empty his life really was. Three days in which he had developed a bond with this woman such as he had never had before. A bond of understanding and trust.

He raked his hands through his hair. If he had the energy he would get up and pour himself a brandy. But telling Grace about his failed marriage had hollowed him out. He felt spent. However, it had also brought a lightness, the lifting of a burden he had carried on his own all this time. Her anger and understanding had touched him deeply. It had lifted some of his doubts and guilt. It had shown him that integrity *did* exist.

He respected everything Grace stood for. With her, there were none of the dramatics of his marriage, which had emotionally and physically drained him. Grace instead was intuitive and supportive.

And physically she drove him to despair.

Tonight, when they'd danced, her body had moved against his like a siren call. Her eyes had held a sexy promise, her mouth the whisper of endless pleasure.

They were both adults. Deeply attracted to one another. Why *shouldn't* they act on it if they were both clear on what the future held?

He stood and made for the stairs.

Grace scrubbed at her teeth, her back to the bathroom mirror. She couldn't bear to see the angry blush that still marred her cheeks.

How on earth was she going to face Andreas in the morning?

A knock sounded on her bedroom door and she leapt in surprise. It could only be one person. She turned and stared into the mirror. What was she going to do?

Her pride yelled at her to ignore him. He had made his position clear. She didn't need any further humiliation.

A second knock tapped on the door...slow and patient...like a man confident she would answer.

On the third knock she stalked to the door and yanked it open. 'Andreas, I'm trying to sleep, to—'

He didn't give her an opportunity to finish her sentence. He marched into the room, shutting the door behind him, and forced her back against the wall. Only inches separated them. He reached out an arm and his palm landed on the wall to the side of her head. He loomed over her, his face taut, his body pulsating with frustrated desire.

His dark eyes devoured hers. 'Did you mean it when you asked me to stay the night with you?'

She tried to answer but his gaze moved down her body and her words were swept away.

'Did you mean it?' His words were a low growl.

'Yes.'

'I can't offer you anything, Grace. We have no future together.'

She ignored the way her stomach flinched at his reminder and looked him solidly in the eye. 'I know.'

His hand reached out and sat on her waist. Slowly he drew her forward until their bodies met. She waited for his kiss, but instead he stayed gazing down at her, his hands following a torturously slow path around her body, sending jolts of pleasure to her core.

He lowered his head and kissed the tender spot at the back of her ear. She gave a low groan.

'You're every man's dream...' He paused to trail kisses along her neck. 'Beautiful, sexy, great legs...' His fingers played with the strings of her pajama vest top for a tantalising moment. 'You smell like a summertime garden in the heat of the midday sun...'

His trail of kisses moved upwards, his stubble dragging lightly across her skin, yet another reminder of his forceful maleness. His mouth hovered over hers.

'And you have the most gorgeous kissable lips.'

With that, he began a slow exploration of her lips that had Grace moaning, her fingers digging into the hard muscle of his shoulders, desperate for him to deepen it.

She was close to tears when he did eventually deepen their kiss, and without warning he lifted her up and wrapped her legs around his waist. Still kissing her, he walked to her bed and together they fell down, Grace crying out in pleasure to feel his weight upon her.

The following morning Andreas woke suddenly, when the bed shuddered hard and banged against the wall.

'Oh, that hurts...ouch...my knee...' At the foot of the bed Grace hobbled on the tiled floor, quietly muttering some low expletives.

'Are you okay?'

She jumped when he spoke, and whispered, 'Sorry, I didn't mean to wake you. I couldn't see in the dark and whacked my knee against the bedpost.'

Andreas sat up further in the bed and switched on the bedside lamp. They both turned away from its glare. A hand over his eyes, he asked, 'Why are you dressed? It's still dark.'

'I need to make a start on the bouquets and finish off the other prep work.'

'What time is it?'

'Five.'

'*Five!* We didn't go to bed until two...to sleep before at least four. You can't function on less than an hour's sleep.'

She reached down and massaged her knee. 'I'll be okay. I have to go.'

The anxiety in her eyes told him that she wasn't going to listen to reason. He would have to resort to other tactics.

'Fine. But not until you come here and give me a kiss.'

She pondered his request with a frown, but then walked over and dropped a quick kiss on to his cheek.

She went to move away but he wrapped his arms

around her and pulled her down onto the bed. He rolled her over him and wrapped his legs around hers, holding her prisoner. She glared at him and he gave a small chortle.

'What are you doing?' Her voice was a breathless low whisper. She pushed against him, but already desire was flooding her eyes.

His fingers dipped beneath her sweatshirt and into the waistband of her jeans. Her body jerked against his.

'Grace Chapman, were you just about to leave without even saying goodbye?'

'No!'

'You're not a very convincing liar.'

'I told you—I have to get to the flowers.'

'And *I* say that you need some sleep. So, whether you want to or not, you're staying here with me.'

She pushed hard against him.

He shook his head. 'You'll have to try harder than that.'

For a moment she considered him. But then she nodded her acceptance and he felt her body relax into him. He gave a low groan when her hand reached round and stroked along his spine. Her mouth, hot and warm, trailed kisses on his chest. Every cell in his body stirred.

His eyes closed of their own volition and he murmured into her hair, 'You're not playing fair. We're supposed to sleep.'

Her hand moved to his belly. His eyes popped open. He inhaled deeply when she gave him a dark, sultry look. He untangled himself from her and flipped onto his back, already lost to her touch. But while he was turning Grace flipped around too—and hopped out of the bed.

He caught her just as she was about to make for the door. He pulled her back into the bed beside him and wrapped his arms around her. 'That was a dirty trick if ever I saw one.'

At first she smiled, with a look of guilty conscience, but then the smile faded, to be replaced by a troubled expression. 'Andreas, please.'

His gut tightened. He ran his fingers lightly against her cheek. 'What's the matter?'

'I'm worried the flowers aren't right. That I've forgotten something.'

'The flowers are perfect. And with your military-style planning you can't possibly have forgotten anything. The most important thing now is that you get some sleep.'

Her breath floated against his skin in broken anxious waves. 'When I woke earlier it suddenly hit me that the wedding is *today*. I don't feel ready.'

He held her tighter to him. A hand gently stroking her hair, he whispered, 'Everything's going to be okay. Sleep until seven. Then I'll come and help you with the prep work.'

She arched back and her violet eyes searched his. 'Are you sure?'

'That I want to be a florist's assistant? No. But I'll do it for you.'

To that she gave a small smile. 'Really?'

'Yes, really.'

They stayed locked together in that position for the longest while, staring into each other's eyes. Her lips lifted into a breathtaking grin and she whispered, 'Thank you.'

A surge of protective desire tore through him, so strong he was momentarily stunned. He kissed her, deeply and intensely, and she responded in turn. They kissed as though their lives depended on it. He ripped her clothes from her. His head spun at the feel of her soft round curves again and he inhaled her scent.

He went to flip her onto her back, but she fought against him. She pushed *him* back onto the bed instead, and when they joined together he stared up into those violet eyes and his heart cracked open at the sight of the honest passion and warmth in her endless gaze.

Grace woke later to the sound of her name being called softly, a hand stroking her hair. She opened her eyes lazily and found Andreas crouched down beside her at the side of the bed. Freshly showered, he wore nothing but a towel wrapped around his waist. He was so delicious she gave him a crooked smile. He smiled back, those green eyes flecked with gold and dancing with…contentment?

'It's six-fifty.'

She gave a lazy nod, her body languid.

'Take a shower and I'll get breakfast ready.'

She swallowed against a dry throat. 'Thanks, but I need to go straight down to the workshop. I won't have anything.'

He raised an eyebrow to that. She thought he was about to argue, but then he gave a small shrug. 'Fine, I'll go and get dressed in my room. I'll join you at the workshop in a little while.'

As he walked towards the door she had a sudden impulse to shout out, to tell him not to go. Not to leave her.

On shaky legs she made her way to the bathroom. Soon afterwards she stood under a scalding shower, her mind racing as her body gave up constant reminders of the intensity of her night with Andreas. A night full of passion and tender moments.

Her head dipped when she remembered that she would be leaving in two days. The hot water battered her neck.

She gritted her teeth and clamped down on all thoughts of the future. It was futile. Sofia and the wedding needed her full attention today.

Ten minutes later she hesitated by the terrace door. She should leave immediately for the workshop, but the rich aroma of coffee and the draw of seeing Andreas again pulled her in the direction of the kitchen instead.

Barefoot, he wore navy shorts and a pale pink polo shirt, his back to her. She hovered at the door, weak with sexual attraction. She longed to go and run her hands through his damp hair, to tousle it, kiss that warm mouth, feel the pulse of his body when he pushed against her.

He turned with a lazy grin and beckoned her over to the breakfast counter. Her legs went weak.

'I should go to the workshop.'

'Come here. Now.'

It was lightly said, but the fire in his eyes told her it was an order—not a request.

When she reached him his hands landed on the waist-band of her jeans, just above her hip bones.

'*Kalimera*…good morning.'

Her insides melted at the low, sensual tone of his voice. He lifted her up to sit on the countertop.

As weak as water, her resistance was only a low gasp. 'What are you doing?'

He gave her a wicked smile and, with one hand remaining on her knee, stood between her legs and reached along the countertop. He pulled a bowl towards them. He dipped a spoon into the bowl and brought up a spoonful of sinfully creamy Greek yogurt and glistening golden honey.

'I'm going to feed you. You have a busy day ahead of you…' He paused and a mischievous glint danced in his eyes. 'And you just had an exceptionally intense night.'

His eyes stayed glued to her mouth when she opened it, the tip of her tongue nervously running along her upper lip. She opened her mouth even wider and squirmed on the countertop as an explosion of tart yogurt and sweet honey hit her palette, but a groan of pleasure managed to escape.

'That tastes *so* good.'

Andreas dropped the bowl to the countertop. *'Thee mou!'* He pulled her towards him, wrapping her legs around his waist.

His mouth tasted of freshly ground coffee, warm and safe. His kiss, at first light and playful, deepened as his hands reached under her sweater and moved up along her spine, around to dance on her ribcage and then over the lace of her bra.

He broke away and spoke against her hair. 'This is impossible.'

She could only agree. With him, she lost all sense. Forgot everything she'd said she wanted in life.

'I know...'

He pulled back and traced his thumb along her cheek, his eyes sombre but tender. 'We need to be careful today.'

She moved to the side and hopped off the countertop. 'Of course.'

'We don't want anyone jumping to the wrong conclusion about our relationship.'

He was right—but that didn't stop her heart plummeting to the floor. She busied herself pouring a cup of coffee from the cafetière. 'Absolutely. Last night was a one-off. I think we should just leave it at that.'

When he didn't respond she glanced in his direction. His arms crossed on his chest, he asked, 'Are you saying that you don't want anything else to happen between us?'

'Aren't you?'

'When you leave on Monday where are you travelling to?'

Uncertain as to why their conversation had taken this direction, she frowned before she answered. 'I'm taking a ferry to Chania, in Crete. There's a renowned wedding florist based there; I'm taking a two-day course at his school next week.'

'Crete is a beautiful island...you will have a lovely time there.'

She had to act nonchalant, pretend that this conversation was *not* leaving her floundering as to how Andreas felt about her.

'I was planning on returning to England towards the end of next week, in time for Matt finishing his exams, but I've decided to stay a little while longer.'

She had listened to what he had said about not feeling overly responsible for her siblings. It was time that she started to let them go and began building her own life in earnest.

She sipped some coffee and glanced at him. He was staring at her, deep in thought.

She should go, but an innate reluctance to leave him had her struggling for something else to say.

'How do you feel about today?' He frowned, and she tried to ease the tension between them with a joke. 'Are you *nervous*?'

He inhaled deeply. 'What do you think?'

Of course he was. Her joke backfiring, she gave him a tight smile. Could she have been more insensitive? After everything he'd told her last night.

'Sorry...of course you are.'

He nodded and poured himself some more coffee.

'I'd better go and start on the bouquets, or at this rate Sofia will have none.'

He glanced at her briefly. 'I'll join you in a little while to help.'

His tone was distracted, with no hint that they had spent the night in each other's arms, sharing a connection so deep that her heart had felt as if it was going to explode with the need to blurt out everything he meant to her.

CHAPTER EIGHT

WITH SOFIA SURROUNDED by the make-up and hair team, Grace slipped out of the bedroom they had taken over in the villa, telling Sofia's mum that she needed to do one final check on the flowers.

She ran all the way down to the workshop. Inside, the room was empty except for the centrepieces and the displays for the reception. While the wedding ceremony was taking place the local florists would take care of positioning them. The centrepieces were even more of a success than she had hoped. Andreas's uncle's porcelain vases emphasised the delicate beauty of the peonies and lisianthus.

Back outside, Grace ran towards the chapel, passing alongside the bay trees and lanterns elegantly lining the path. She smiled at the ribbons floating in the light breeze, but then a dart of pain shot through her heart. *Their time alone was over.* She pushed that thought away. The wedding guests would be arriving in less than half an hour. She needed to make sure all the flowers looked perfect.

As she approached the chapel her heart sank. The floral displays lined the red-carpeted aisle, sitting at intervals between the rows of white wooden seats. But the florists were still attaching the garland to the frame of the entrance to the chapel, and the garland for the bell tower still sat to one side of the terrace.

She rushed forward to help them and together they finished the door garland. At the same time Grace ran through with them the checklist of all the other jobs that were to be done. When she came to the corsages and boutonnières, the two women studied her blankly.

Grace closed her eyes for a second. *She had forgotten to arrange for them to be delivered to the bride's and groom's parties.* The guests would be here soon, and Christos and Andreas would need to be down at the jetty to greet them.

She raced back to the workshop, praying that the carefully constructed cascading curls the hairdresser had created, twisted into a half-knot at the base of her neck and topped with a spray of lisianthus, wouldn't fall apart.

In the workshop she grabbed the corsages and boutonnières and sprinted back to the villa. She heard loud voices coming from the formal sitting room. She gave a light knock and entered.

Christos was surrounded by at least ten friends, all larking about as Andreas helped him into his tuxedo jacket. They all turned as she entered, smiling at her curiously. She went to turn away, certain she had made a faux pas in her intrusion on this male domain, but Andreas's mother—beautiful and elegant in a powder-blue knee-length dress—suddenly appeared, and with an exclamation of delight gave Grace a warm hug.

'*Kalosìrthes!* Welcome, Grace! How lovely to see you again.'

Over his mother's shoulder she briefly caught Andreas's eye before he resumed buttoning Christos's jacket. Her throat closed over at the sight of the intimacy between the two brothers, and when she pulled away from the floral cloud of his mother's perfume she bent to rearrange the boutonnières, desperate to hide the tears filming her eyes. What on earth would his mother think if she saw them?

There was a lot of good-natured jostling between Christos and his friends. Despite his mum's welcome Grace hovered on the outside of the group, awkward and unsure. She understood why Andreas was staying removed from her, in his desire to hide the truth of their relationship, but part of her longed for him to show some form of acknowledgement, some warmth towards her.

His father approached, pouring champagne into a flute, which he forcibly handed to her. 'You are just in time. I'm about to make a toast.' He twisted around and held his glass up high. 'To Christos and Sofia. May they have a *long* and happy marriage.'

A loud cheer went up from the other men and they all moved in to hug Christos, their affection and friendship for the groom clear. Her eyes darted to Andreas as he stepped out of the friendly jostling. His tight expression told her that he too had heard his father's heavy emphasis on *long*.

'Aren't these flowers so pretty? Grace, you've done a fantastic job.'

His mother fussed around her, and Grace instantly knew that she was accustomed to deflecting any potential arguments.

A laughing Christos extracted himself from the group long enough to draw her into a hug. 'Yes, thank you for all your work.' His eyes glinting, he asked, 'What did Sofia say when she saw the flowers?'

Earlier Grace had taken Sofia to the workshop to show her the flowers. Sofia had burst into tears, and a horrified Grace had thought it was because she didn't like them, but Sofia had assured her it was because they all were so beautiful. The bridal bouquet—a hand-tied spiral cloud of pale pink Sarah Bernhardt and ivory Duchesse de Nemours peonies, finished off with a long length of silver-grey ribbon—now sat in pride of place on the bridal suite's dressing table, along with her own smaller version made with the Sarah Bernhardt.

Grace had never seen Sofia as worked up as she was today. And the last thing an already nervous-looking Christos needed was to know that his albeit deliriously happy bride had been shaking like a leaf all morning.

'She loved them and she can't wait to see you.'

Christos gave a grin of relief which grew into a wide megawatt beam: the gorgeous smile of a man in love. Grace had to walk away for fear that tears would fill her eyes again at witnessing this real-life romantic tale unfolding before her.

She took a sip of champagne and dared a glance at Andreas, who had come to stand next to Christos. Both he and Christos were wearing beautifully tailored tuxedos, crisp white dress shirts and black silk ties. They both looked gorgeous…but when she glanced at Andreas memories of last night had her weak-kneed with desire.

He was staring in the direction of the other men, who had moved over to a table of food at the opposite side of the room. But her instinct told her he was attuned to everything she was doing—as though he was on tenterhooks about her letting slip the truth about what they had shared over the past few days.

Flustered, and feeling too hot, she placed her champagne flute next to the flowers on the coffee table. 'I'd better get back to Sofia.'

'Stay and help us fix the boutonnières,' his mother

said, picking up one of the sprays. 'When Andreas got married I couldn't get them to sit properly.'

Then, as though realising what she had said, his mother glanced towards Andreas and then his father in alarm. Christos threw a worried glance at Andreas, who stood rigid, still, tight-lipped.

His father bristled and in a low voice said irritably, 'I thought we'd agreed not to discuss that wedding?'

Grace picked up his mother's corsage and turned her back to the men. Much taller than Mrs Petrakis, she fixed the single ivory-white peony backed with two sprigs of lisianthus to her powder-blue dress and gave her a sympathetic smile. She smiled back at Grace gratefully, blinking hard at the tears in her eyes. Eyes the same green burnished with gold as Andreas's... Though finished, Grace deliberately fussed with the corsage a while longer, until Mrs Petrakis touched her arm gently and nodded that she was okay.

Next Grace attached a boutonnière to Christos's lapel. She gave him a cheeky smile. 'You look incredibly handsome today.'

Christos smiled back in delight. And then he lowered his head and said, for her ears only, 'I'll take good care of her.'

Tears instantly filled Grace's eyes at his tender but heartfelt promise, and for a few seconds she wondered if she would ever meet a man who would be so keen and happy to marry *her*.

She busied herself with selecting the next boutonnière, and then steeled herself to approach Andreas's dad. He glanced down at her briefly, and then looked away. Though not quite as tall as Andreas, Mr Petrakis exuded the same power and strength as his oldest son.

Her fingers fumbled with the catch of the pin and she could feel his impatience growing.

To distract him, but also in a bid not to allow herself to be intimidated by him, she stood up tall and looked him in the eye. She pretended to speak to the four of them as a group, but her gaze remained on his father. 'I'm afraid that I've been a nuisance to Andreas over the past few days, but to his credit he has been courteous and generous at all times. You should be incredibly proud of him.'

Mr Petrakis glared at her impatiently. 'Of *course* we're proud of him.'

Behind her she heard Andreas give a disbelieving laugh. And as she picked up the final boutonniere, Christos chortled and said, 'My brother? Courteous? Who knew? You're mellowing in your old age, Andreas!' Christos threw an arm around Andreas's shoulder. 'But you're right, Grace, about him being generous—he always has been.' Christos looked directly at Andreas. 'Thanks for hosting the wedding.'

Behind her, Mr Petrakis cleared his throat noisily. 'I still don't understand why you wanted it *here*. It would have been so much easier in Athens, rather than dragging everyone out into the middle of the Aegean.'

Andreas's jaw tightened. In an instant Grace wanted to stand up for him. 'I think the majority of people would *love* to marry on this island—it has to be the most romantic place I've ever been. I'd happily stay here for the rest of my life.'

Flustered at the eyebrows rising around her, and the prospect of placing a boutonnière on Andreas's lapel, Grace walked towards him and, thoroughly distracted, said to Christos as she passed him by, 'You must be pleased with Andreas's wedding present?'

Christos stared at her, confused. 'What present?'

Panic soared through her veins and she looked at Andreas in alarm. His jaw had tightened even more, and irritation flared in his eyes.

'I'll tell you later. It was to be a surprise.'

Grace hesitated in front of him. She swallowed hard as a deep blush fired on her cheeks. She gazed up at him and mouthed, *I'm sorry.*

He gave an almost imperceptible shake of his head before looking away. The double lilac lisianthus was perfect against the black of his suit, but her fingers trembled so much she was worried that she'd never actually manage to pin it on. Her head spun from embarrassment, and the effect of standing so close to him. It reminded her of how good it had been to have those arms around her, being free to inhale his scent all night long, the way his body had dominated hers, the sensuality of his lips, his mouth...

Behind her, his father said, 'Well, if Grace knows about the present, then I think there can be no reason why *we* shouldn't.'

Grace froze. Beneath her fingers Andreas's chest swelled as he inhaled a deep breath. She pulled away just as he spoke, his tone sharp.

'Later.' He checked his watch and turned to Christos. 'We should go down to the jetty—the first boats will be arriving soon.' As though to punctuate his words, the sound of a helicopter overhead reverberated through the air.

His father walked towards the door. 'I'll go and greet the guests coming by helicopter.'

All the men disappeared from the room. Grace tried to ignore the way his mother was studying her and quickly made her excuses and left the room too.

She climbed the stairs and stood outside the bridal

suite for a while, inhaling some deep breaths. How could the man who had looked at her with such impersonal detachment just now be the same man who had made passionate love to her last night? Had whispered private words of endearment.

He had made her feel as though she was the centre of his universe, but right now she felt as if she had been cast out of his world.

Beside him Christos jigged nervously as they waited for Sofia to arrive. The late-afternoon sun was dipping low behind them, casting shadows on the terrace. In front of them Grace's flowers looked like giant balls of marshmallow—the perfect romantic finishing touch to what even *he* had to admit was an incredible wedding venue.

His skin itched even at the thought.

He took a glance backwards to check for Sofia's arrival and caught his father's eye. Since he had arrived a few hours earlier his father had once again managed to push his every button. The same old grievances about how overworked he was and how lucky his friends were to have sons who gladly took over the family business. A none-too-subtle reminder of how this island should have been his all those years ago. And several digs as to how he hoped *this* marriage would last.

Andreas gave Christos a quick, encouraging clasp of the shoulder. 'She'll be here soon. She can't change her mind and run away too easily on an island.'

He had to forget his father, forget his past, and concentrate on making this day special for Christos.

'Cheers, brother, that's really reassuring.'

The two brothers grinned at each other and then Christos ducked his head down so that no one else could hear their conversation. 'So what's this about a wedding present?'

Emotion thickened Andreas's throat and it was a while before he managed to speak. 'The paperwork is in my office... I'm giving you half of this island.'

Christos studied him, speechless. 'Seriously?' he said at last.

'Yeah, seriously.'

The two men embraced and then stood side by side in silence. Eventually Christos spoke, 'We had great times here as boys, didn't we?'

Andreas nodded. 'And we'll have them again.'

Christos looked as though he was about to say something, but just then the sound of traditional music reached them. The trio of musicians, playing violin, bouzouki and the *toumbi* drum, would have led the bridal party all the way from the villa to the chapel.

Sofia was the first to appear behind the musicians, on the arm of her father, her dark hair covered in a lace veil. Beside him Christos inhaled a deep breath, and Andreas couldn't blame him. Sofia was radiating elegant beauty and happiness, her eyes dancing, her mouth a wide beam. And when her eyes met Christos's a single tear trickled down her cheek and Andreas had to turn away. He felt as though he'd been punched in the gut.

He tried not to look back but was unable to resist doing so. When he did, he knew he should look away, but he couldn't. His breath had been knocked out of his lungs. Her head slightly bowed, a smile playing on her lips, Grace followed Sofia. Her silver-grey dress was made of fine lace on the bodice, and a full-length tulle skirt. Silver sandals were on her feet. Was she wearing the underwear he had unpacked? And was it truly only twelve hours ago that they had lain together, their bodies entwined and damp with perspiration?

He forced himself to turn. Already he had seen his

parents' curiosity as to what was going on between them. His mother constantly searched for any sign that he was in a relationship again, hoping against hope that one day he would have a family of his own. It would be unjust and cruel to mislead her.

He stared at the peonies cascading down from the garland around the chapel bell. He had helped Grace place the peonies in flower tubes this morning. He had thought then that he could trust her. Had thought so last night. But within minutes of meeting his family she had hinted at the personal nature of their relationship by revealing that she knew about his wedding present to Christos. Was she playing him? Trying to back him into a corner?

His stomach twisted at the thought that he might have been duped once again.

When Sofia reached Christos she raised her hands to his and they stared at each other for long moments, before they drew into each other, their noses touching. Together they grinned and turned to the congregation, who broke into spontaneous applause at how infectious their joy was.

The priest eventually managed to draw the wedding party into a semicircle, so that he and Grace were practically facing each other as they flanked Sofia and Christos. While their eyes would briefly meet, and then fly away from one another, in contrast Christos and Sofia never stopped gazing into each other's eyes, lost in one another.

What was Grace thinking? Was she dreaming of her own wedding? When her eyes landed on him did she imagine *him* in the role of her groom? Panic surged through him. Surely not? He had made his thoughts on marriage clear. But last night they had shared an extraordinary intimacy. One that in truth had rocked him to his core. What if she had felt that intensity too? What if he had given her false hope?

When it came to the time for exchanging the rings, he heard Christos's words of reassurance to Sofia, whose fingers were trembling so much he found it hard to slip the ring on her finger. Immediately Sofia stilled, and the couple shared a look intense with understanding and care. Andreas's gaze moved to Grace. She was staring at Sofia and Christos with tears glistening in her eyes. And then she was looking at him, as though asking him a question.

He glanced away. His heart sank. He had no answers for her.

The whoops of joy from the other guests when the newly married couple kissed for the first time transported him back to three years ago, when a similar whoop had echoed in an Athens cathedral. He had been so blind.

He looked back into the congregation. So many of those faces had witnessed his own marriage. How many still speculated as to why his marriage had gone bad so quickly? Why he no longer spoke to one of his closest friends.

His gaze met his mother's. She gave him a sympathetic smile of reassurance. He glanced away and pulled at the collar of his shirt. He needed a drink.

When they followed the bride and groom down the aisle Grace's hand barely touched his arm. They both smiled, but tension kept their bodies rigid as the crowd shouted, *'Na zisetel!'*—Live happily!—while showering the procession with a mixture of confetti and rice.

Before them, Christos and Sofia stopped at the edge of the terrace, where they would greet each of their guests before moving on to the reception. The couple were tied in an intimate embrace and Grace's footsteps faltered.

'I'm sorry about earlier.'

Andreas turned around to see if anyone was close by before he replied. 'I said that we needed to keep our relationship private.'

The volume of the voices around them increased, and Sofia's soft laughter ran through the air at something Christos had whispered to her while in their embrace.

Grace moved closer to him. 'I know. I wasn't thinking.'

It would be so easy to believe her—especially when her eyes pleaded with him to do so. He stepped back. They were standing way too close together. 'My parents are now speculating as to why I told *you* something so personal.'

Grace peered up at him with hurt in her eyes, but didn't respond. He led her over to stand next to the bride and groom, so that they too could greet the guests and be on hand in case they were needed. He felt torn in two.

Unable to stop himself, he leaned down briefly and whispered in her ear, 'You look beautiful.'

She studied him, confounded, and then looked away into the distance, tears in her eyes.

Andreas began to exchange hugs and handshakes. The happiness of everyone else was pulling him apart—along with the guilt of knowing that last night with Grace had been a major mistake.

Out on the Aegean the sun had long disappeared in a spectacular sunset of fiery pinks when the main courses of grilled swordfish and mouthwatering lamb *kleftiko* were finally cleared away. The wedding reception was proving to be a loud and fun affair, with numerous toasts and shouts for the wedding couple to kiss.

In other circumstances Grace would have been able to relax at this point, knowing that the flowers had proved to be a huge success, with many favourable comments. But not only did she have Andreas's father sitting next to her at the top table, as the day progressed she was feeling more and more alienated from Andreas.

The tapping of a knife-edge on a glass had her glancing along the table. Andreas stood and the terrace grew silent. He threw the crowd a devastating smile, but she could see tension in the corners of his eyes. She held her breath as her heart pounded. *Please let this go well for him.*

He spoke first in Greek, and then after a few sentences stopped and translated into English for the guests from England. At first he spoke about the tricks he had played on his younger brother when they were children, with Christos eager to believe everything his older brother and idol said. And then of what Kasas had meant to them both growing up. He told them about their joint adventures, including a failed entrepreneurial attempt to start breeding goats, in which the stubborn animals had proved much too temperamental for the young teenagers. And then, his voice thick with emotion, he said how happy he was to see Christos marry here today.

Beside her, Grace could feel Andreas's father tense.

He went on to compliment Sofia on how radiant she looked today, which drew a large applause from the crowd. And then he faltered. For the longest while he stared down at his notes.

Grace shifted in her seat, her stomach clenching, her heart thundering as she willed him on.

He pushed his notes away. 'I was told that I shouldn't wing my speech, which was probably good advice—but as my father will tell you I'm pretty stubborn when it comes to taking guidance.'

This drew knowing laughter from some of the crowd

and friendly heckling. At first Mr Petrakis sat frozen, but then he gave a nod of acknowledgement and said, 'Whoever hurries stumbles.'

Andreas and Christos shared a look that said they had often heard that expression before, and then Andreas continued. 'Firstly I must compliment Sofia's chief bridesmaid, Grace, who is also the florist for today. Having seen first-hand the work involved, I must admit to a whole new appreciation for the skill and dedication required.' He raised his glass and said, 'To Grace.'

His eyes met hers for the briefest of moments before he turned away. Grace smiled in acknowledgement of the guests toasting her and shared a hug with Sofia. Inside she felt as if she was going to die. She hadn't expected him to say anything about her, and that would have been preferable to the impersonal way he had just done so. As though they were nothing but mere acquaintances. Where had the fun and the friendship between them gone?

'Passion can spark a relationship, but it can't sustain it. Aristotle described love as being a single soul inhabiting two bodies. Christos and Sofia—that is my wish for you: that you share the same dreams, the same values, have a common life vision. These are the things that keep a couple together.'

Grace bent her head and closed her eyes on the emotion in his voice, swallowing against a huge lump in her throat.

'May you for ever be a single soul, living a life of shared dreams that allows your love to take root and blossom with each passing year.' Then, raising his wine glass, he invited the guests to join him in a toast. 'May your love blossom.'

For the rest of the speeches Grace sat trying to listen,

forcing herself to smile and laugh when others did, but feeling numb inside.

As soon as the speeches were over she made her excuses, while the terrace was being cleared of tables for the dancing, and went to check that all the lanterns were lit on the lower terraces and on the path down to the jetty. She tried to stay focused on her work, refusing to think about Andreas's speech and the obvious implications for them as a couple when they didn't share a single dream.

When she eventually returned to the terrace the music had started.

Sofia rushed over to her. 'I was searching for you! It's time to dance the Kalamatiano.'

Sofia pulled her out on to the dance floor, along with her mum and Andreas's mum. They all held hands and were soon encircled by a large group of female wedding guests. The music started and they began circling the dance floor, using small side-steps. The music was infectious, as was Sofia's happiness, and for a while Grace lost herself in the joy of the dancing, in the endless smiles of the women facing her.

But then she spotted Andreas where he stood beside Christos, watching the women dance. The two brothers couldn't have appeared more different in their expressions. Christos was laughing, his eyes glued to Sofia, while Andreas just stared at her for a moment, his expression devoid of any emotion, before he turned away to talk to a group beside him.

He said something to a striking dark-haired woman and stepped closer when she laughed. Something pierced Grace's heart. She felt like doubling over as jealousy and pain punched her stomach with force.

Memories of her father's voice taunted her. *'You need*

to toughen up, Grace. Your looks are fading as quickly as your mother's did.'

As they twisted and circled around the terrace, the high spirits of everyone around her, the beauty of the candlelit terrace bathed in the scent of jasmine, mocked everything in her.

What had she expected? She had known what she was getting into. One night of fun—nothing else. But as she watched his dark head bend, saw him talking to the woman whose eyes were shining at being on the receiving end of his attention, she knew it had never been that simple.

CHAPTER NINE

'COME AND TALK to Giannis.'

Andreas gritted his teeth and turned at his father's call. He reached out to shake Giannis's hand, but was pulled into an enthusiastic hug instead.

'Good to see you, Andreas. I haven't seen you since...' Giannis's voice trailed off.

His father tensed beside him and Andreas answered deliberately, in a casual drawl, 'Since my wedding.'

Giannis gave him an uncomfortable smile and obviously decided to change the subject. 'I've been following your successes in the business pages.' He paused and glanced to Andreas's father. 'You must be enormously proud of Andreas and everything he has achieved.'

His father frowned, as though he wasn't certain either of the comment or how to respond. He eventually brushed off the comment with a dismissive wave of his hand. 'Of course, of course...but now it's time for Andreas to come back to the family business. Like all good sons would do.'

Andreas didn't want to hear any more. He made his excuses and walked away. Out on the dance floor, the party was in full swing. He should be enjoying himself. But in truth he just felt frustrated. Frustrated and angry. He had sat through Christos's speech with pain and regret burning in his gut, knowing he would never have the same dream for the future, the vision of having a partner for life, children, a family of his own.

This wedding was a constant reminder of his own failings. And now his eyes fixed on his greatest frustration of all. *Grace.*

She was out on the dance floor with his cousin Orestis. They were standing much too close to one another. A cut-out section in her dress exposed her upper back. It was the sexiest thing he had ever seen, and images of his mouth running the length of her spine last night almost knocked him sideways.

They had shared so much last night—physically and emotionally. At the time it had felt right, but now he was questioning everything about it. It had left him feeling exposed, and with emotions so conflicting that he couldn't even begin to process them in the madness of the wedding.

His cousin was a charmer and a heartbreaker. He marched right over.

'Whatever Orestis is telling you, don't believe a word of what he's saying.'

Orestis stood back from Grace and raised an eyebrow. 'Well, I *did* learn everything I know from you, cousin.'

Beside him Grace's lips twitched. Andreas didn't like the feeling that it was him against the two of them. Grace was supposed to be on *his* side.

'Not everything Orestis… I'm not a heartbreaker.'

His cousin squared up to him, Greek male pride refusing to back down. 'True, but from what I hear you don't hang around long enough to be one. You don't break hearts—you just steal them.'

Grace looked from Orestis to him and back again.

'Two peas in a pod, I would say.' She walked away into the crowd.

He caught up with her in the centre of the dance floor as the band moved to a slower tempo. 'I've been neglecting my best man's duty to dance with the chief bridesmaid.'

Angry violet eyes damned him. 'Thanks, but I'm not in the mood.'

She went to walk away but he pulled her around and into his arms. His frustration with the whole damn day boiled over and he lowered his head to her ear. 'You weren't so reluctant last night.'

Her foot stamped on his. He held back a groan and tightened his grip. Her body squirmed against him, her heat and scent sending thunderbolts of desire to every sensitive point in his.

He glanced up in time to see some speculative gazes been thrown in their direction. He took a step back but kept a firm grip on her, in case she decided to bolt. With a false smile he warned, 'If we don't dance, people will be even more suspicious of us.'

She gave him a frustrated glare and said through clenched teeth, 'I don't care what people think of us.'

'Really? So the next time we meet you don't care if everyone is wondering about us? Hoping that we get together?'

She hesitated for a moment. 'They won't.'

'Look around you, Grace.'

She gave an indifferent shrug. 'I just see women staring at you and looking as though they would love for *me* to disappear off the face of the earth.'

'And beyond them are my aunts and uncles, my parents, hoping that one day I will marry again.'

'Would that be such a bad thing?'

It was a question he didn't even want to entertain. 'We're not going over that again, are we? You know how I feel.'

The anger in her eyes disappeared. 'I know. I just hate the thought of you going through life on your own.'

Her comment hit a raw nerve and he tried to bite down on the anger coiling in his stomach. 'Not everyone needs a fairy-tale ending to be happy.'

She gave him a long, hard stare. 'As long as you *are* actually happy.'

He wasn't going there.

Inch by inch they moved towards one another. His hand touched the bare skin of her back. He had to swallow a groan as he felt the smoothness of her skin, the delicate ribbon of her spine, the slender span of her waist.

'I haven't seen much of you today.'

He glanced down in order to understand the true meaning of her comment. Her wounded expression had him looking away quickly. A surge of defensiveness followed. 'I've been busy talking to all the guests. I haven't seen many of them in a number of years.'

She didn't respond, which only upped his frustration a notch. Was he messing up *everything* today? He needed to get them back on neutral ground. Grounds of friendship. If that was possible.

'Many guests have spoken to me about how incredible the flowers are; you must be pleased.'

She threw him a dirty glare and said with a note of sarcasm, 'So you said in your speech.'

He'd felt all day as though he was under attack—from memories, from others' expectations, from his own stupid pride. He was sick of it, and his defensiveness surged back at her comment. 'You didn't like my speech?'

For a while she glared at him, and then the fight

seemed to leak out of her. 'No, it was a perfect speech. Funny, heartfelt, kind…just like you.'

He gave a disbelieving laugh. 'That's not how many people would describe me.'

'If you let them into your life they would.'

'Maybe I don't *want* to let them in.'

A small shrug was her only response. Her breasts moved against his shirt and he pulled her a little closer. He was unable to hold back a low groan at the feel of her body pushed against his.

Her voice was unsteady when she spoke. 'Are you enjoying the day?'

He could take no more.

In a low growl he answered, 'Not as much as last night.' His pulse went wild when he pulled back to see the heat in her eyes. 'Let's go somewhere private.'

Grace followed him into the villa, wondering if she was losing her mind. It was as though she was addicted to him and to what he could do to her body.

The villa was empty, and at the bottom of the stairs he took her hand. Upstairs, he pulled her down the corridor and into a dark room. In the moonlight she could see a bed in the far corner.

'Where are we?'

'My bedroom.'

'Is this a good idea?'

'Of course not, but you started it.'

And she had—last night, when she'd asked him to stay the night with her.

In the near darkness his eyes blistered with need, pinning her to the spot. Her body was already on high alert to him, tense with building desire. His head lowered even closer…his hand lightly touched against her neck. She gave an involuntary shiver and a small cry of frustration.

His mouth hovered over hers. 'You do crazy things to me… Do you realise just how beautiful, how sexy you look today?'

She shook her head, unable to speak as her body cried out for his mouth, for the pressure of his weight.

'Are you wearing that lingerie I unpacked?'

He spoke in a low, demanding whisper, his lips agonisingly close to hers, pulling every nerve in her body exquisitely tight.

She was incapable of doing anything other than giving a simple nod.

He gave a primal groan and his mouth landed heavily on hers. His hands clutched the sides of her head, so that he could deepen the kiss even more. His mouth was familiar, but wondrous, hot, seeking, relentless. Her hands ran down the hard thick muscle of his outer chest, over the indentations of his ribs.

She gasped when his hands dropped to work on the buttons of her dress.

She should pull away. But she didn't care. She wanted him. *Now.*

Her dress fell in a puddle to the floor and he stepped back. His eyes devoured her. A powerful jolt of desire rocked her body as she saw his hunger, his ravenous appreciation of her almost naked body. His head dipped to her breasts, his lips running along the curve of exposed flesh cupped by the bustier. His hands trailed along the delicate flesh of her inner legs. With a groan he twisted her around to face the wall and ran his hands over her bottom. The weight of his body pushed against her.

He dropped his head down to her ear. 'I can't get enough of you.'

A tremor went through her at his low tone and suddenly, for some unfathomable reason, she was unable to stop shivering.

Behind her, he stilled. And before she knew what was happening her dress was being pulled back up and he was closing the buttons.

Too confused to speak, she waited, her body a mess of desire and unstoppable tremors. Buttons finished, he twisted her back towards him. He said nothing, but ran a hand through his hair, frustration clear in his expression.

'What's wrong?'

His mouth was a tight grimace. 'We can't do this again. I was wrong to bring you here.'

Just like that, he was shutting her out again. She had no idea what he was really thinking. Why had he suddenly decided to push her away?

Humiliation clawed in her chest. 'Tell me the truth, Andreas. What's going on?'

He gave a frustrated sigh. 'The truth? The truth is we should be downstairs with the others...and I like you too much to hurt you again.'

Confusion built thick and fast in her chest until it ached. His words were bittersweet. She didn't know how to respond. All she knew was that a ball of rejection had been growing inside her all day. For the past little while it had shrunk, whilst they had danced and kissed, but now it was a giant boulder inside her, weighing her down, consuming her.

The last time she had felt so rejected had been when her mum had told her that there was no hope of them ever being a family again.

Feeling lonelier than she had in a long time, Grace walked away, terrified that she was about to start crying in front of him. Downstairs, before she walked back out to the terrace, she glanced backwards to see Andreas following her, his head bent as though in defeat.

Andreas stared out onto the dance floor, knowing he had two choices. He could either walk away from the celebrations now, in an attempt to try to pull his head together. Or he could forget about everything and embrace the wild momentum of the party.

It was an easy choice.

He walked onto the dance floor and was pulled into the dancing.

The pace and communal elation, the sheer goodwill, numbed him to the emptiness inside him. He joined Christos and their mutual male friends. Wasn't this camaraderie and friendship enough?

And then the floor cleared and he was pushed forward to perform the *zembekiko*. He resisted the pushes from the other men. It was a hot-blooded dance that demanded that all emotions, all weaknesses be expressed. To dance the *zembekiko*, the manly dance of improvisation, you had to be unafraid of expressing the true you...and right now he didn't know who he was.

The guests were crowding around the dance floor, some kneeling, others standing, all urging him forward. He still resisted. To do this dance right he would need to expose his feelings of pain, of unfulfilled dreams. The crowd would think of his failed marriage. He would think of the future that had been wiped out the moment he had opened the blackmail letter and seen those photos of his wife.

Sofia was moving through the crowds, pulling Grace behind her, and they dropped to the floor in front of all of the other guests.

The band began the low plaintive music. He glanced

towards Grace. She returned his gaze with eyes heavy with sadness.

He moved to the centre of the room. He would dance for her. It was the only way he could reveal what was in his soul.

Andreas stood in the middle of the dance floor, proud and dignified. He stared into the distance, his broad shoulders tense, his arms flexed. His tux jacket had long disappeared and his shirtsleeves were rolled up.

He started the dance with slow, deliberate movements, his leg bending in a fluid movement upwards so that his hand tapped his heel. He circled the dance floor, assured and noble, ignoring the crowd who were calling out his name and clapping to the beat of the music.

Grace clapped blindly, her heart beating heavily in her chest.

His movements intensified, growing ever quicker, and he dipped and twirled, lost to the rhythm of the music. His movements were strong, but they held sadness, loneliness. He was all alone out on the dance floor, with the world looking in.

Suddenly she wanted to go to him. Wanted to comfort him as his body stamped out a message of despair. But she sat there, her hands clenched, her heart aching, as he spun around, his hand whirling down to slap the floor. The crowd shouted out whoops of approval. Tears filled her eyes. Sofia reached for her hand. Together the best friends watched this powerful man dance with passion, his focus only on expressing the emotions within him. His aloneness.

The dance ended abruptly. Andreas walked straight off the dance floor towards Christos, his gaze never meeting hers. The crowd erupted into loud applause.

Beside her Sofia gave a soft chuckle and exhaled loudly, wiping her eyes. 'Wow, I feel worn out! That was incredibly moving. I've seen the *zembekiko* danced many times before, but never with such raw emotion.'

Grace could only nod, her throat much too tight to utter even a few meaningless words. She stared at Andreas's back as he stood silently amongst a group of friends, wanting to go to him, to place a hand on his arm, on his back. To be with him. To be part of his life. And in that moment she knew that she was in love with him.

She closed her eyes and winced. She couldn't be. He wasn't what she wanted. He didn't want a relationship, or romance in his life.

Beside her Sofia stood and held out her hand to Grace. As Grace stood, Sofia whispered, 'Are you okay?'

She could not burden Sofia with her problems. Anyway, what had happened between her and Andreas was too personal, too private. She doubted she would ever tell another person about what they'd shared. *Ever.* It was a secret she would hold in her heart for the rest of her life.

She forced herself to smile. 'I think it's just culture shock—weddings in England are so much more tame in comparison to this... I hadn't realised Greek weddings were so passionate.' She paused and gestured around her at the dancers back out on the floor, the large groups laughing and hugging, dancing with abandon as though there was no tomorrow. 'And so much fun.'

Sofia tugged her out onto the dance floor, where they joined Sofia's beaming dad. He twisted and twirled them around the floor and Grace tried to forget about the man standing in the crowd behind her, who had stolen her heart.

It was well after midnight when the band leader called Sofia and Christos to the stage. With the encouragement of the crowd Christos knelt down and helped Sofia step out of her shoes. He lifted them up to Sofia and together they inspected the soles.

Earlier that morning Grace had watched Sofia write the names of all the single woman attending the wedding onto the soles, as was tradition. Now it was time to reveal the names that were still visible on the soles—the women whose names still showed would be the next to marry.

Sitting with a group of Andreas's family, Grace watched, bemused, smiling at the hopeful girls and women eagerly waiting for their names to be called out. It seemed she wasn't the only romantic in the world.

A dart of pain shot into her heart and she glanced towards Andreas, who was seated at a table with a group of fellow young and beautiful Athenians. He was engrossed in conversation with another man, oblivious to her. The group seemed so effortlessly chic and full of vitality. Inadequacy crept along her bones. She touched a hand to her hair, fixed her dress, wishing she had taken the time to check her make-up.

Sofia gave a squeal that echoed into the microphone. It hooked everyone's attention and conversations died as they all focused on the stage.

Christos stepped closer to the microphone and spoke first in Greek and then in English. 'There's only one name remaining.' He chuckled when Sofia gave another squeal of excitement, and stepped back to allow her to speak.

Sofia scanned the terrace. When her gaze landed on her, Grace stared back, fearing her heart was about to give way. *Oh, please, would someone tell her that Sofia hadn't included her name. She didn't want attention... this number of eyes on her.*

Sofia held up the shoe. 'The only name remaining is… my bridesmaid, Grace!'

All two hundred guests turned to study her. Her heart leapt with joy for a few insane seconds, but then she pushed it away. Heat fired through her body. What was she supposed to do? Stand up and wave? Make a speech? Protest and say that it had to be a mistake…that she was the most unlikely woman to marry…that she had just fallen in love with a man who didn't want to be in a relationship, never mind marry?

She grimaced at Sofia, silently warning her best friend that she would get her back for this. Sofia responded with a defiant grin. Grace squirmed, and wished that people would stop staring in her direction. Her cheeks burnt brightly. Vulnerability swept through her and she wished she was anywhere but here. She forced herself to smile; to do otherwise would be churlish. She didn't dare peek in Andreas's direction.

His aunts made cooing noises of appreciation around the table, and his mother translated for her. They were saying that it would soon be Grace walking down the aisle, as hers was the only name remaining. His mother watched her curiously and she squirmed even more into her chair.

'That's very unlikely.'

His mother translated her response back to his aunts but it was greeted with frowns and shakes of their heads. His mother didn't need to translate their words contradicting her disbelief and she sat there, dumbfounded, wondering how she had ended up in this surreal mess.

The dancing resumed and she exhaled in relief when her five minutes of attention faded. She took a sip of her white wine and glanced towards Andreas. He was staring directly at her. His expression was impossible to pin down…thoughtful…frustrated…hacked off.

He needed to know that she gave no significance to the shoe tradition. That she thought it was a silly bit of fun.

She approached his table and threw her eyes to heaven. 'Well, *that* was embarrassing.'

'Was it?'

'Lord, yes…your aunts are predicting a wedding before Christmas.' She shrugged and laughed, but clearly Andreas wasn't finding it funny.

He gave her a brief, impersonal smile—the kind of smile that passed between strangers. Then he stood and gestured for her to sit on his chair. He introduced her to the others at the table and said, 'I need to go and speak to some of the other guests.'

He walked away.

Grace sat there, randomly smiling at the people around her, trying to pretend that she didn't feel as if she had just been punched in the chest…trying to convince herself that he hadn't just blown her off.

CHAPTER TEN

GRACE ADJUSTED HER sunglasses against the glare of the afternoon sun as it bounced off the body of the helicopter and forced herself to smile and wave enthusiastically, saying goodbye to Sofia and Christos. Her throat felt as raw as sandpaper and her eyes burnt with tears.

A sharp wind whipped around her as the helicopter blades picked up speed and she backed away, glad to have an excuse to move away from Andreas who had also come to the helipad to say goodbye to the honeymoon couple.

As soon as the helicopter was in the air she gave one final wave and walked away. Andreas caught up with her on the main terrace, now restored to its original state after yesterday's wedding reception. The terrace, as with the rest of the island, both so full of chatter and merriment yesterday, now felt empty and forlorn. All the guests had left over the course of the night and this morning. Only she and Andreas remained.

'Come and have some lunch.'

She turned at the brusque nature of his invitation. Was this the same man she had slept with, shared so much intimacy with, less than two days ago? Not trusting her own voice, she shook her head and went to follow the path back down to the workshops.

In an instant he was at her side and pulling her to a stop. He regarded her curiously. 'Are you okay?'

Even the brief touch of his fingers on her arm made her resolve to stay away from him waver dangerously. 'I'm fine...'

'You obviously aren't. What's the matter?'

'I'm just upset that Sofia's gone. Yesterday went too fast, and this morning...' Grace paused and willed herself not to blush. 'I didn't get to speak to her for more than five minutes.'

They both knew that the reason this had been the case was because the honeymoon couple had been holed up in their bedroom all morning.

Andreas looked unconvinced by her answer. But before he could ask any further questions she turned again for the workshops, where she had already spent the morning tidying away all the floral displays from yesterday, glad to have a reason to avoid Andreas.

Not once had he spoken to her again after the 'name on the sole' debacle last night. In fact he had barely even glanced in her direction.

She had gone to bed long before the party had ended, heart-sore and mentally shattered. At first she had fallen into an exhausted sleep, but had woken with a start to hear a female giggle as the dawn light had crept between the shutter slats. She hadn't dared move when she had heard Andreas's voice. *Was he with another woman?* The voices had quickly moved on and she had resisted the urge to peek out of her window. She was humiliated enough without adding the role of jealous lover to her repertoire.

Back at the workshop, she busied herself removing the peonies from the long length of garlands. She hesitated when Andreas appeared at the door, but forced herself not to react.

'Did you clear away all these flowers yourself?'

She glanced up at the astonished tone of his voice. He gestured to the peonies Grace had brought back to the workshop during the course of the morning, and then pointed down to the jetty.

'And the pots and lanterns? Who brought all of those back to the jetty?'

'I did.'

He glared at her incredulously. 'By yourself? What time did you start working this morning?'

'At seven.'

'The wedding didn't end until sunrise. What's the rush? I could have helped you if you had asked.'

She stared at him pointedly. 'I went to bed at two. I had plenty of sleep until I was woken by voices at dawn.'

His mouth twisted and he folded his arms on his chest.

Memories of last night felt like a red-hot poker sticking into her heart. Hurt swelled inside her. 'I've decided to leave Kasas today, so I needed to start the clean-up early. Ioannis says he can take me over to Naxos for the five o'clock ferry.'

For a moment he looked stunned, but then his eyes narrowed as though he didn't quite believe her. 'You're leaving today? Why?'

'Do you *really* need me to answer that, Andreas?'

He moved closer to the workbench and bent down to meet her eyes, his eyes boring into hers, his jaw working. 'I wouldn't ask unless I needed to.'

She turned to throw some peonies that were shedding their petals into a composting bin. Her chest ached; she could barely draw in enough breath. The composting bin was starting to fill up and she studied the dying peonies with regret. Their time of beauty was much too short.

She turned and faced him with her head held high, determined she would maintain her dignity. 'I'll be blunt. We slept together Friday night and you ignored me all day yesterday.'

'No. I didn't ignore you. I told you we had to be careful that people didn't get the wrong impression.'

'And what other people might believe is more important than hurting me?'

He gave a disbelieving shake of his head. 'I hurt you? How?'

'You shut me out completely.'

He threw his head back and stared down at her with that arrogant expression he sometimes used. 'You're exaggerating.'

His tone reminded her of her father's belittling attitude. Fire burnt through her veins. 'Really? You barely looked at me all day, never mind actually *talked* to me. I thought I meant a little more to you than that... And I deserve a little respect.'

'Maybe if you hadn't blurted out about knowing what my wedding present to Christos was we wouldn't have had my mother watching us like a hawk all day, wondering what was going on between us.'

Grace marched over and grabbed a cardboard box from the floor. At the bench she began to pack her floristry equipment into it. Without glancing up, she said angrily, 'It seems to me like you were looking for an excuse to push me away.'

'Why would I want to do that?'

She knew she should stop—that she was only hurting herself. But a force inside her—an emotional force she didn't fully understand—pushed her to lash out, even though the rational side of her yelled at her to stop, that she was going too far.

'I don't know. Maybe you regretted Friday night? Perhaps revised your opinion of me because I was the one who suggested it? Maybe, facing your family and friends, you suddenly realised that I was lacking? After all, I'm just a florist—which is pitiful compared to your career. And I certainly don't stack up against the women who were only too keen to grab your attention yesterday. Like the dark-haired woman in the white trouser suit. Was it *her* you were with this morning out on the terrace?'

Andreas moved forward and pushed the cardboard box away, so that nothing stood between them other than the table, which he leaned on in order to eyeball her at a closer range. His eyes were dark with fury.

'Yes, it was. Her name is Zeta and she's my cousin. Orestis's sister, in fact.'

'Oh.'

His lips twisted and he growled, 'And I do *not* regret Friday night. Do you?'

She could barely breathe. In a small whisper she admitted, 'No…'

'What do you want from me, Grace?'

She wanted to go back to what they'd had on Friday night, as they had lain in bed together. That emotional and physical connection. A connection so deep and right and secure. She wondered now if it had all been a dream. How could they have gone from that to this so quickly?

'I thought we were friends.'

He exhaled loudly in irritation. 'Friends don't sleep together.'

'Yes, they do…married couples are best friends to one another.'

He stared up towards the ceiling and rubbed a hand

down over his face. 'I forgot what a romantic you are. All of this was such a bad idea. What were we *thinking*?'

He sounded worn out. She should stop. But the force deep inside her was driving her on, wanting to test him. Wanting him to admit what was in his heart. That, yes, he *was* pushing her away. Closing himself off from her and everything that they'd shared.

'I don't know...what were *you* thinking? Was I just another conquest for playboy Andreas Petrakis?'

He walked away from her and stood at the door. His body was rigid, his hands balled at his sides.

It was a while before he turned and said coolly, 'I am not going to dignify that with a response. Why do I feel you're trying to back me into a corner, here? I have always been honest with you. I told you that I could never give you the type of relationship you wanted.'

He was right, in a way. She *was* trying to back him into a corner—but not to try to manipulate him into a relationship with her. No, what she wanted was him to tell her out loud that it was over, that the connection they had shared had been of no consequence to him. That without a backward glance he would walk away from her.

'I know... I just wish I hadn't fallen in love with you.'

He felt as though someone had punched him. Every fibre of muscle in his chest constricted painfully. His ears rang. Nothing made sense.

He looked away from the pain in her eyes. He had to get away before he did something stupid. Something he would regret for ever. Like taking her in his arms and making her promises he could never fulfil.

He sucked in some air. 'I wish you hadn't said that.'

She flinched, but said nothing.

His chest felt as if it was about to explode. He walked closer, his eyes never leaving hers. 'Why did you?'

Her eyes held his for a few moments. She was clearly bewildered by his question. And then they grew wide with shock. 'You think that I'm *lying*?'

'Are you?'

She stood stock-still, only her eyelids blinking, a thousand thoughts flashing in her violet eyes. Eventually he saw a grim determination take hold and she stared at him coldly. 'No, I wasn't lying. But if you can think that I'm capable of doing so, maybe I was wrong.' She paused, her hands gripping the side of the workbench. 'No, I'll rephrase that. Not *maybe*. I *was* wrong. I can't possibly be in love with a man who can think that I would lie about something so important.'

He didn't want her to be in love with him—and yet her words twisted in his gut. 'Your love seems pretty fickle if you can change your mind so rapidly.'

'Maybe you've just revealed your true self to me... Don't blame me for falling for your pretences.'

'What pretences?'

'That you trusted me, respected me enough to show me kindness and consideration. Yesterday just proved that you never truly did trust or respect me.'

'Oh, come on! That's utter rubbish. Yesterday I had responsibilities that needed my attention. I was the host and the best man. I had to speak to the other guests. I'm sorry if that made you feel neglected. Added to that, I had my family breathing down my neck. Why on earth are you blaming me for trying to protect you from years of my family wondering what happened between us and if anything will happen again? Do you honestly want that speculation? That pressure? You heard Christos. He wants us all to meet here in August for a family get-together. Christos sees you as *family* now, Grace.'

Her shoulders sagged. 'I know. And somehow we need to try and get on. Put these days behind us.'

Her voice now held sad resignation. Her anger he could handle; this pain was unbearable to witness.

She reached for some floristry wire and twisted it in her hands. 'We have to put some distance between us. That's why I must go today.'

'I do respect you…and I've always been honest with you.'

'But you're not even honest with *yourself*, Andreas. How can you possibly be honest with me? You've put a barrier up against the world because you were hurt before. You put on this mask of being hard-headed and cynical. But deep inside you are kind and lovely. Or at least I thought you were. Right now I don't know who you really are. Maybe even *you* don't know.'

'Are you suggesting that I *don't* learn from my past? From my mistakes? If you take that path, Grace, you'll be hurt time and time again. Maybe being cynical and tough is the only way to survive this world. Maybe those barriers will help me thrive. And are they any different to the romantic dreams you hold…? Aren't they a barrier in themselves? Will you ever meet your ideal man? Or will you realise we are all made with feet of clay?'

About to drop a spool of wire into the box, Grace paused and peered at him with a distracted expression, deep in thought. Any remaining fight in her seeped away.

'Maybe you're right.'

She went into the adjoining room, returned with a sweeping brush and began to clean the floor. Exasperated, he walked out of the workshop, his fear of ever really trusting a woman battling with the desire in his heart to turn around and take her in his arms and make this mess go away.

Later that afternoon Grace sat on the side of her bed and stared down at the blank page of her notebook. She wanted to write him a note but didn't know where to start. She didn't even know if it was the right thing to do. Maybe she should go and speak to him. But her heart plummeted to her feet even at the thought.

She was in love with him. And it was so wrong. She wasn't supposed to fall in love with a man who was cynical about love, who could shut her out with such ease, with such indifference as he had shown yesterday. Unfortunately she knew that there was another side to him—a man who was fun and attentive, kind-hearted and tender. A seductive, powerful man who made her melt just by looking at her.

But he didn't love her.

In truth she had no idea what he *did* feel for her. Friday night, when they had made love, she'd thought he felt the same strength of connection. In the moonlight he had lain with her, his eyes holding hers, filled with the same happiness and amazement that had flowed through her. She had thought his feelings for her were as deep and profound as hers for him.

How could she have got it so wrong? And why were a hundred different emotions chasing her down? One minute she was in shock, the next close to tears, the next wanting to yell at Andreas and demand to know what those tender words he had whispered to her in Greek when they made love had meant. Because to her they had sounded like declarations of love.

What was she going to do about August? Sofia was

moving to Athens with Christos next month, and had been so excited about inviting Grace to join them here on the island for holidays. Sofia would be hurt if Grace said no. Perhaps she should promise to come next year instead. But then would she just be putting off the inevitable? Would it be even harder to face Andreas next year?

A small voice in her head mocked her, goading her weak resolve, pointing out that she couldn't possibly bear not to see him for another year.

'Ioannis is waiting for you out on the terrace.'

Her head shot up to find Andreas standing at her bedroom doorway, his sombre expression only adding to his unfair good looks. He propped a hand against the door frame, his burnt-orange polo shirt riding up to expose an inch of muscled torso above the band of his faded jeans. Her pulse thundered even faster.

She shut her notebook and stood. 'I'm ready to go.'

His eyes moved to her suitcase and to the weekend bag beside the dressing table. He nodded, but didn't say anything.

She gripped the notebook. So much adrenaline was coursing through her body that despite her legs feeling weak and shaky she was possessed with a burning need to run. To run out of the room, to run away from the gut-wrenching desire to touch him again, to feel his lips on hers.

She placed the notebook and pen into her weekend case. 'I have already told Ioannis, but just so that you know, the florists from Naxos are coming tomorrow to take away the floral supplies, and they will reuse the peonies for a church.'

Again he nodded, but didn't say anything. She grabbed her suitcase and walked towards him. He didn't move. She forced herself to give him a tight smile, her eyes darting over his face quickly, instinctively knowing that to linger would spell trouble.

Tension crackled in the room. Even a few feet away from him she felt the tug of his body. Her eyes blinked rapidly as she tried to ignore the pull of memories: the weight of his body, the overwhelming power and strength of his hold.

In a low voice he said, 'I meant what I said last night. I do like you. A lot. And I never meant to hurt you.'

Distress coiled in her chest, in her throat, blocking off her airways. He went to place a hand on her arm but she stepped back. If he touched her she wouldn't leave here with a shred of self-respect intact.

Though she had never wanted more to run away, she forced herself to speak. 'Thank you for everything you did to make yesterday so special for Sofia.'

'Will you tell Sofia?'

How could he ask her that? Did he know her at *all*? 'Of course not.'

'Why not?'

Now she definitely wanted to yell at him. Yell at him that she wouldn't betray his trust, that she couldn't possibly reveal what they had shared, the awful soul-wrenching beauty of it, even to her best friend. Disappointment invaded every cell in her body.

'Why? Are you going to tell Christos?'

'Of course not…but women like to share these things.'

'Why *wouldn't* you tell Christos? Maybe then he would understand if we were tense when we're together. In fact, maybe we should tell them. And then they might do the sensible thing and keep us apart as much as possible.'

Grace was staring at him with wild eyes, a slash of anger on her cheeks. What was he *doing*? Why did he have such a burning need to prove that he couldn't trust her? It was like a monster inside him, consuming him. He hated himself for it. But it was out of control.

'I'm hoping the next time we meet the heat will be gone out of our relationship.'

She jerked back. The blood drained from her face. 'The heat?' She grabbed her suitcase and made for the door.

If he hadn't stepped out of the way he was certain she would have shoulder-charged him. As it was, the wheels of her suitcase rolled over his toes.

He cursed and ran after her. He yanked the suitcase out of her hand. 'I'll carry it downstairs for you.'

She grabbed it back. 'No. Just back off, Andreas. *I don't need you.*'

Her biting words felt like fingernails clawing into his heart. He followed her down the stairs.

She walked out to Ioannis on the terrace and called to him in a happy voice. Then she turned to him. He'd expected a scowl, but she gave him a bright smile. Only the tremble in her hand when she reached it out to him told of her pretence.

'Thank you...' For a moment she paused, as though uncertain as to how to continue. 'For your help with the flowers.' Affecting a breezy air, she added, 'I'll see you again in August. It will be lovely to spend some time with Sofia.' Her tone was cool and distant.

He needed to let go of her hand, yet he held on to it. He felt her trying to tug it away but his fingers clasped tighter. 'Enjoy your time in Crete.'

Tears shone in her eyes and her smile quivered for a moment. 'I can't wait.'

CHAPTER ELEVEN

FOUR DAYS LATER Grace sat at a waterfront bar on the horseshoe-shaped historic harbour of Chania city. Around her tourists ambled in the early-evening sun, soaking in the architecture and beauty of the Venetian harbour, stopping to inspect the menus at the vibrant restaurants or to step into the craft shops that lined the waterfront. Behind the harbour, on one of the criss-crossing narrow lanes, lay her hotel, one of many boutique hotels located in the restored town houses of the Venetian quarter.

Her floristry workshop had finished an hour earlier, and while part of her had wanted nothing more than to go back to her room and collapse onto her bed, she had forced herself instead to make the most of her time in this pretty city. To ignore how her heart bent in two every time a couple passed her.

This city seemed to do something to people. It was as if its romantic laid-back atmosphere insinuated itself into everyone's mood. Couples held hands and whispered intimacies to one another. Families sat at café tables and chatted for hours on end. And Grace was so lonely she felt physically ill with the pain tearing at her heart, the empty pit in her stomach.

But she could not let it defeat her. For the past few days she had stared that loneliness in the face, and as small chunks of realisation had formed into a larger understanding she had slowly begun to make sense of her past. And why Andreas pushing her away had hurt so much.

A couple passed in front of the bar, bent into one another, laughing and teasing, hands tucked into each other's sides as they tickled one another. She glanced away and grabbed her wine glass. She lifted it to her mouth but put it back down untouched. Blindly, she pulled out some coins from her purse and left them on the table.

On the cobbled street of the waterfront and in the side laneways she kept her head down, navigating the crowds, racing away from memories of how Andreas had pulled her back into bed that Saturday morning and held her hostage with teasing and tickles—a prelude that had quickly led to the most shattering of lovemaking.

Her hotel was tucked along a narrow lane in the middle of a stacked terrace of four-storey town houses. The reception was a simple hallway that daylight only touched early in the morning. In the evenings the owner—Ada, warm and generous—lit a row of candles that beckoned her guests in.

Grace climbed the wooden stairs to her bedroom on the top floor, hearing the now familiar sound of her own footsteps on the worn threads and smelling the scent of furniture polish. The higher she climbed the more sunlight penetrated the windows as the town house crept out of the hold of the neighbouring properties.

On the landing turn of the top floor her eyes met the sight of familiar polished tan shoes. She stumbled against the banister. Shoes she suspected were handmade. Especially for him.

Her heart started. Was she seeing things in her sleep-deprived state?

She saw dark navy trousers, tanned hands gripped

tightly between bent legs as he sat on the top step of the stairs, a pale blue shirt and then his broad shoulders, muscled neck, sharp jawline, the hint of an evening shadow. Her eyes lingered on his mouth and she was assailed by memories of intimate moments, but also afraid to move them upwards. What would she find there?

She gripped the banister and peeked up. Her heart stopped. Deep shadows filled his green-eyed gaze; lines of tension crinkled the corners of his eyes.

'Hi.'

Such a simple word, but said gently and with a small smile it conveyed so much more. But was that just wishful thinking on her part?

The butterflies in her stomach and her leaping heart swooped together to form one mass of confusion in her chest. She stumbled out a stunned, 'Hi...'

His smile slowly died and they stared at each other. The air crackled with the tension of intense attraction and hurt.

He rested his arms more heavily on his legs and leaned towards her. 'How are you?'

She tried not to grimace and met his eyes. 'I'm okay.'

He studied her doubtfully and rolled his neck from side to side, as though trying to rid it of tension. 'For the past few days I've been trying to convince myself that I was okay with you leaving. That you would never be part of my life. But today I flew home to Kasas, after a few days of business in Budapest, and realised just how lonely the island was without you.'

Her heart leapt and hope fired through her. But then reality jumped in and gave her a stern talking-to; he was here because of the sexual attraction between them—nothing more.

A slash of embarrassment coloured her cheeks. 'I'm not interested in a fling.'

His expression hardened. 'Neither am I.'

'So why are you here?'

He twisted around on the stairs and turned back to her holding the messiest bunch of hand-tied Coral Charm peonies she'd ever seen. He held them out to her.

She examined them dubiously. 'Where on earth did you get those from?' The florist who had put the bouquet together should hang her head in shame.

'I went to your floristry school. They told me you had already left. I wanted to bring you some flowers so I bought these there.'

'Somebody in the school created *that*?'

He looked indignant. 'No, *I* put it together—and I thought I did a pretty good job, considering.'

'Why?'

'Because I wanted to show you what you mean to me—if that means faffing around with flowers and embarrassing myself in front of a group of strangers who seemed to find it all very amusing, then so be it.'

Her head spun. This whole conversation was getting more unreal by the moment. 'How did you even know where I was? I didn't tell you the name of the school or what days I would be attending.'

'Sofia told me.'

He was the one who'd wanted to keep their relationship secret. Sofia would definitely suspect something now. 'Didn't she want to know why?'

'Yes, and I told her that I had messed up big-time and needed to find you to apologise.'

'But what about keeping our relationship private?'

'Finding you was more important.'

He spoke with such quiet intensity it left her unable

to draw breath, never mind find an adequate response. She took the bouquet from him and ran her finger and thumb along the fragile petals.

He gestured to the narrow confines of the stairs and the nearby bedroom doors. 'Can we talk somewhere more private? In your bedroom?'

Her budget had only allowed for a single room. Avoiding physical contact with him in such a small space would almost be impossible. She shuffled uncomfortably. 'It's a tiny room—nothing like the hotel rooms you would use. There isn't much space.'

His gaze narrowed. *'Aman!* Do you think I care about what size the room is when we have so much to talk about? Heaven help me, but if we have to have this conversation in a broom cupboard we will.'

Andreas stood and waited for Grace to pass him on the stairs. Beneath the top layer of the delicate fabric of her tea dress she wore a rose-pink slip, the borders covered in a deep pink lace... He was like a teenager around her—staring down her dress at the exposed slopes of her breasts, fantasising about undressing her.

With a tiny huff she flew past him. His hands itched to reach out and grab her. To feel her body against his again, to inhale her summertime scent, to feel her gentle breath on his skin.

She opened her hotel room door with an ancient key and went immediately to the balcony doors at the opposite side of the room and flung them open.

Yes, the room was small, but it was filled with her scent, and for a moment he couldn't move with the sensation that *this* was where he belonged. Surrounded by her scent, by the scattering of jewellery and make-up on the dressing table, the sight of her clothes in the wardrobe, her shoes below, a lone white and crimson bra hanging on a chair-back.

How was it possible that he adored every single item that belonged to her? Longed to hear when and why she had bought them? He wanted to bury himself in her, heart and soul. Know everything about her.

His head reeling, but more than ever determined to right the wrongs he had committed, he joined her out on the small balcony, which only had enough space for them both to stand.

'Great view.'

Beside him she leaned on the railing, her back arching. Her loose hair swung down to the sides of her face so that he was unable to see her. He longed to push it back, to be able to see those eyes, that full mouth again.

'You wanted to talk.'

Where would he start? His heart leapt wildly in his chest. Fear balled in his throat. He dragged in some air. Through the neighbouring rooftops the harbour was visible. His eyes ran along the harbour wall to the lighthouse at the end. His stomach rolled. He had to explain. But what if the damage he had done was irreparable?

'When my ex cheated on me it changed me.' He paused as humiliation raged through him.

Grace straightened beside him and studied him fleetingly. 'Because you loved her?'

Her quietly spoken question hit him hard in the gut. He gave an involuntary wince. 'The fact that you have to ask that question again tells me just how much I've messed up.'

She rested against the balcony railing and waited for him to continue, watching him warily.

'I wasn't in love with my ex. My feelings for her never came close to what I feel for you. The pain of my divorce was because of my pride. My father had warned me against marrying my ex and I ignored him.'

Unable to face her while saying what needed to be said, he turned and stared instead at the red clay rooftop of her hotel.

'A year later he was looking at photos of my wife, naked with another man. The paparazzi had sent the photos to him too, in a bid to blackmail him. It tore me apart to see his humiliation and disgust.' His stomach rolled again, and he clenched his hands into tight balls. 'We have our differences, but he didn't deserve that.'

On a soft exhalation, Grace said, 'How awful...' Her hand reached out for a moment to touch his arm, but then she pulled it back, crossing her arms on her chest instead. 'Did you talk about it?'

Boy, had they. He gave a bitter laugh. 'Well, he yelled at me non-stop for an hour, about the disgrace I'd brought to the family. And then all the old arguments resurfaced: how I had walked away from the family business, taken sides with my uncle.'

'But he couldn't blame you for your ex's behaviour?'

'He had warned me about her. After we argued my father and I didn't speak until Christos's engagement.'

'And that hurt you?'

More than he had ever imagined. 'Yes. He's stubborn and pig-headed, but in his own way he loves me. The day he passed that envelope of photos to me he seemed broken. Until he lashed out and spoke of the disgrace it had brought to the family name. My wife had cheated on me. So had a close friend. I felt like a failure. My pride had taken a huge dent. The only way I could cope was to throw myself into work and pretend that I didn't care.'

'What about your mum?'

'She was heartbroken and stuck in the middle, trying

to negotiate peace between us. Family is everything to her. She said nothing, but I could see with my own eyes her upset. I'd made it clear that I would never be in a relationship again. And of course that meant that I would never give her grandchildren.'

'Andreas, why are you telling me this?'

'My refusal to trust others again was because of shame and wounded pride. I refused point-blank to believe that I could ever trust in a woman again. I was convinced of it. It gave me safety and security, I would never be humiliated again. I would never endure the pain of being betrayed. And then *you* walked into my life. Loyal, generous, fun, giving. You. I hated how attracted I was to you. I tried to fight it. But I became more bewitched by you every time we were together.'

She stared at him, clearly confused, before walking back into the bedroom. There she sat on the side of the bed, its vibrant yellow bedspread a golden sun in the otherwise neutral bedroom with its white walls and recycled furniture painted in shades of white. She rubbed a hand along the nape of her neck, her head dipping so that he couldn't read her expression when he sat on the chair opposite.

She brought her hands together on her crossed knees and squeezed so tightly her unvarnished fingernails turned white. 'But you didn't trust me.'

'Before the wedding, as I got to know you, I *did*. It was the only reason I came to you on the eve of the wedding. I trusted in you. With me, with Sofia, with your family, you are supportive and strong. You don't play games. You don't try to manipulate others for your own ends. You're honest and loyal.'

Her hands flew up into the air. 'You didn't think that

on the day of the wedding. It was clear you didn't trust me then.'

He grimaced, but nodded his agreement. 'I'm not proud to admit that I panicked. Our night together, the morning after…it blew me away. It was different to anything I'd experienced before. I was falling for you and it scared me. You wanted love and romance. I couldn't give you either. At least I thought I couldn't.'

'I honestly didn't mention the wedding present deliberately. I'm so sorry that I did.'

'I know you didn't. You said the day after that I was looking for a reason to push you away. And you were right.'

Grace bowed her head and ran a hand over her face. Without seeing her expression, he knew he had hurt her again.

In a rush he continued. 'Not just because I saw that my mother suspected something was happening between us, but because the whole day was bringing back memories I had refused to think about since my divorce and I couldn't cope with them.'

'Why didn't you explain any of this to me?'

'Because I didn't even want to acknowledge it to myself. I just wanted my life to go back to the way it had been before. Comfortable and easy…never risking myself personally. I didn't want to fall in love and risk being hurt, being humiliated again, so I just jumped from date to date. And tried to convince myself that it was enough. But then I met you, and instantly I was falling for you, and it scared me to death.'

'Why were you so scared?'

'Because I once had a future mapped out for me. With a wife and children—my own family. And when that dream turned into a nightmare I decided that love and relationships were for fools. That it wasn't worth the risk of being humiliated, failing again.

'I thought I was against Christos marrying Sofia because they barely knew each other, but the reality was I hated having to face everything I'd lost—my dreams of having a loving marriage, children, a woman who would be my best friend.

'At the wedding Christos and Sofia's happiness mocked everything I had tried to convince myself didn't matter to me. And I was also trying to deal with the intensity of my feelings for you. I couldn't deal with how I was feeling: the pain of remembering a future that had been torn away from me, the memories of shame, my damn pride, and how I—a cynic—was falling in love with a woman who wanted to be swept off her feet.

'I just wanted it all to go away. It was all utter madness. I didn't know what to do, so I pushed you away. But for the past few days I've been the unhappiest I've ever been. You've changed me. You've made me look inside myself and realise just how lonely I was before you came along; how empty my life was with its endless work and partying. I'm tired of living a pretence.

'Seeing how courageous you are in helping your family, in what you said to me on Kasas before you left about not being honest with myself, I realised I needed to let go of my shame and humiliation. That I was letting my pride get in the way of ever loving a woman again.'

Though his stomach was churning, Andreas forced himself to admit it. 'The wedding was like an X-ray of everything that was wrong in my life, and because I didn't like what I saw I messed up. And I'm here to say I'm sorry.'

Andreas's apology had tumbled out in a rush of heartfelt words. It was going to be so hard to say no. Even now, with her heart shattering into smaller and smaller fragments of pain, because she knew the reality was that they could never be together, she wanted him with a desperate ache that was tearing her apart.

'You're not the only one who messed up on the wedding day. For the past few days I've been trying to understand why it hurt me so much that you were so distant, and I've realised it actually had very little to do with you.'

He leaned towards her, those broad shoulders tensing under the cotton of his shirt. 'What do you mean?'

She closed her eyes at the memory of her forehead resting on the solidity of his collarbone, the sensation of his chest rising and falling beneath her cheek. Regret and guilt washed over her.

'I was expecting too much from you. I should have seen that you were struggling and supported you, instead of constantly looking for signs that you were pushing me away. You had told me about the pain of your marriage, about your relationship with your father. I should have stepped back and given you the space you needed, but instead I was almost willing you to push me away because I knew it was inevitable. Deep down I wanted it to happen sooner rather than later... I was already in love with you, and I couldn't bear the thought of falling even more in love with you only for you to end it all.'

'Why was it inevitable?'

'Because you told me time and time again you didn't believe in love and relationships. And, let's face it, you aren't exactly the romance-loving guy I plan on marrying.'

'Maybe I could become a romantic?'

'I suppose miracles do happen.'

For a moment they shared a smile, and she wondered how she would manage to walk away from him.

'But there was another reason why I thought it was inevitable.' An awful, giddy light-headedness came over her and she had to pause to try and right the world, which had tilted for a moment. 'It happened with my mum.'

Her words came out in a bare whisper. It had taken every ounce of strength in her to force them out. It was as though her heart had been clinging to them, afraid it might shatter if she spoke them publically.

'And if she could do it so could you.'

Andreas moved forward in his seat so that their knees were touching. He laid a hand gently on her leg. Those green eyes held hers with a compassion so great she had to glance away in order to speak.

'All through my childhood it was me and my mum against my dad. To me, we were a team, protecting Matt and Lizzie against him. We never spoke about it, but we instinctively worked to take them out of his way when he was about to let loose about something. One year, when it was Lizzie's birthday, he came home at the end of her party and there was a huge argument about the house being a mess. What had been such a fun and happy summer's day instantly became dark and terrifying. He started shouting. He decided Lizzie should be taught a lesson for allowing her friends to mess up the house and lit a bonfire to throw her presents onto it. My mum rushed Lizzie and Matt upstairs, before they knew what was happening, and I hid as many presents as I could before locking myself in my room.'

'How old were you?'

'Eleven.'

'You were too young to be dealing with that.'

'Perhaps, but at the time it just felt like it was part of life—and I had my mum on my side. But then one day I came home from school and she had left us. I couldn't believe it. I was convinced my dad was lying. I thought he had hurt her. He wouldn't tell me where she had gone.

Eventually he told me out of spite, during an argument. She had moved home to Scotland. I spent a whole day travelling to see her. I wanted to make sure she was okay. Check when she was going to come home. But she wasn't ever going to come home. And when I begged her to allow Matt and Lizzie to come and live with her she said no.'

'Grace, I'm sorry.'

He edged a little closer and she took comfort from his nearness and the sincerity in his eyes.

'What did you do?'

'I buried my feelings and tried to forget everything about her—the relationship we'd had, that she even existed. I put all my time and energy into Matt and Lizzie. On the wedding day, because you were so distant, all the fear and pain of my mum walking out on me came rushing back and I couldn't cope. Added to that, I was missing Lizzie and Matt. And with Sofia getting married... I guess I just felt extra vulnerable because the people I love were moving on.'

She dragged in some air, tears of regret filming her eyes.

'I'm sorry I wasn't there for you more. I can understand now why you might have thought I was backing you into a corner.'

He came and sat beside her, his hand skimming against her cheek before tucking a strand of hair behind her ear. 'I promise I'll never leave you. *Ever.*'

What was the point in him saying that? They had no future.

'I want you in my life, Grace. I know I have been far from your ideal man, and that I haven't swept you off your feet, but I want to make up for that now. I want to take you on dates, visit Paris and Vienna with you, watch the Bolshoi Ballet, take you hiking in the Pindus Mountains.'

She could not help but smile. 'That sounds lovely, but I now know that I don't need any of that. Ever since my mum moved out I've built up this idea in my head that a great romance would fill the void she left. I thought that was what love was—grand declarations of love, the heady whirlwind of being swept off your feet, the surface romance that has no roots. Now I know it's something much more profound. It's trusting and respecting one another. It's about feeling secure and loved. In those hours before the wedding we *did* have that together, didn't we? In those hours I stopped feeling alone because of you. And that's all I want from love. Nothing else matters.'

For a moment he said nothing, but then a steely determination entered his eyes. 'Marry me.'

What? Where had that come from? He wasn't playing fair. This was close to torture.

'Marry you?'

'Why not? I don't want to lose you. And what better way can I prove to you that I trust you?'

How could he ask her to marry him when he didn't even love her?

'Andreas, I can't marry you just because you want children, a family of your own. I love you, but I'm not going to compromise. I want a man who's passionately in love with me.'

He regarded her with astonishment. 'Can't you see how in love I am with you?'

Her bottom lip wobbled. 'You *love* me?'

'Of *course* I do. I fell for you the moment Christos sent me that photo of you pulling a silly face. As crazy as it might sound, I looked into your eyes and fell in love with you even before I met you. I love everything about you. Your ambition…your loyalty. The fact that you love Kasas as much as I do. How kind-hearted you are. I've never been so attracted to a woman in my life. And it's killing me to think that I might spend the rest of my life without you, not able to see your smile, hear your voice, touch you. Make love to you. I need you in my life.'

Punch-drunk, she tried to buy time to let everything he said sink in by teasing him. 'Andreas Petrakis—is there a romantic soul lurking behind that tough armour you wear?'

'Yes, and if you agree to be with me I promise to show you every day of our lives how much I adore and cherish you.'

He was in love with her.

She tightened her fingers around his, her heart dancing in her chest. 'I'm sorry about not supporting you, doubting you. I love you so much, and I want to be with you for ever too, but for now I'd like us to spend time together, to have some fun without pressure or expectations. I want to have our first proper date, our first trip to the movies, our first summer together. To simply be girlfriend and boyfriend for a while. What do you think?'

With a single move he lifted her up and sat her on his lap. He began to nuzzle her neck and in an instant she was putty in his hands. Her eyes rolled as his lips moved along her skin, his mouth warm, his teeth playfully nipping.

In a low, sizzling voice he said beneath her ear, 'I'll go with it—for now. But I'm never going to let you go. I need you in my life.' And then, pulling back, those green eyes burning with love, he added, 'My helicopter is waiting at the airport; are you ready to come home to Kasas?'

She cradled his head in her arms and buried her nose in his hair, inhaling the lemon scent of his shampoo.

'What were the words you whispered to me when we made love?'

Love shone in his eyes when he lifted his head. '*Psi-himou*—my soul.' His hand cradled her cheek. 'Through your love and kindness you have freed me to believe in dreams again.'

Her mouth an endless smile, she kissed him.

EPILOGUE

THE PALE LATE-AFTERNOON winter sun warmed Grace as she sat on the step outside her hillside flower shop on Naxos, sketching in her notepad. A month after opening and she still got a thrill every morning when she arrived to open up. *Her shop.* She had done it. She was running her own wedding floral design business and florist. All financed by the money she had earned designing and supplying flowers for weddings throughout the islands during the past summer—thanks to the incredible publicity following Sofia's wedding.

In the large shop window she had placed an old bicycle, its yellow paint fading, the front wicker basket filled with an abundance of vivid orange and yellow gerberas. Overhead hung a mix of pale wooden hearts, crafted locally from driftwood. Behind the window display Grace had kept the shop simple: pale green walls, Andreas's uncle's ceramics positioned in the various nooks and crannies of what had once been a bakery, and simple teak wooden tables and counters for displaying the flowers… roses, calla and oriental lilies, alstroemerias, chrysanthemums, euphorbia, bear grass and bamboo spirals all sitting in a mismatch of flower containers.

The sound of footsteps on the cobblestones had her pausing as excitement tingled through her limbs.

It couldn't be. He wasn't supposed to be home until the end of the week.

She wanted to look up, but the fear of being disappointed had her instead staring blindly down at her sketches. But as the footsteps came nearer and nearer goosebumps erupted on her skin and she held her breath as a sixth sense battled with logic.

It's not him. It's only wishful thinking.

Polished black leather shoes came to a stop in front of her. *Andreas!* Her heart leapt into her throat.

'*Yassou, psihimou.*'

The widest, daftest grin broke on her mouth at the sound of his low greeting. Her eyes shot upwards, taking in the charcoal trousers, matching suit jacket and light grey shirt, open at the collar. A grin played on his lips, and his eyes held hers with a mischievous delight.

Pleasure and excitement sent waves of heat into her cheeks. 'You're home!'

'Yes, I'm home.'

Her heart tumbled. 'I thought you weren't coming until the end of the week?'

He sat beside her, and though her head spun at being so close to him, inhaling his distinctive addictive scent of spice and lemon, she forced herself not to touch him, enjoying these moments of teasing tension too much.

'I cut my visit to the Caribbean short.' With a playful frown he added, 'I had no choice but to do so as I missed you so much.'

She frowned too, pretending not to understand what he was talking about, when in truth the past five days without him had felt as though she had lost a part of herself. 'But we spoke at least three or four times a day.'

He shifted on the step, so that his knee touched against the cotton of her red trousers. He leaned in towards her.

'Yes, but I couldn't touch you, bury my mouth against your throat, run my hands over your body, make love to you.'

Her toes curled in pleasure at his low, sexy growl. For a moment she closed her eyes as the delicious desire which had been building inside her from the moment his helicopter had left Kasas last weekend almost made her fall apart there and then.

She cleared her throat. 'And I thought you were with me for my stimulating conversation…'

His hand enclosed her knee, and he gave it a squeeze before his thumb began to circle against the much too sensitive skin on the inside of her leg. She inhaled a ragged breath, and he gave a satisfied grin before he replied, 'I'm with you because every morning I wake smiling, knowing that you are in my life.'

Oh, God, she was about to cry.

'I missed you so much.'

'Not as much as I missed you.'

That wasn't possible.

She shook her head. 'I doubt that.'

His eyes challenged hers good-humouredly. 'Oh, really? I could barely concentrate in meetings… I lost my appetite. I couldn't stop talking to people about you or sleep at night, even though I slept with your nightdress.'

She tried not to giggle. 'You slept with my *nightdress*! Which one?'

'The dark raspberry one that drives me crazy every time you wear it.'

'The nightdress you bought for me in Vienna?'

'Yes. I stole it from the side of the bath before I left on Saturday morning.'

They both paused as they remembered how he had dragged a sleepy Grace into the shower with him that morning, peeling her nightdress from her body and tossing it away, and how quickly she had awoken to his touch.

She sat for a minute, drinking in the beauty of his face: the strength and pride of his high cheekbones and arrow-straight nose, that mouth that in an instant could make her forget everything but him, the wonder of his eyes that constantly held her in his grip.

'I love you so much, Andreas. It scares me a little. What if I ever lost you?'

He moved forward and his lips landed on her cheek. It was a light kiss, a tender one. And it was followed by a train of similar kisses of reassurance across her cheek to the shell of her ear. Grace arched her neck as her heart exploded and desire coiled in her belly. His breath was warm, his lips firm.

Against her ear, he whispered, 'I will always be at your side. I would lose everything I own, cut off my right arm, rather than ever be without you. You are part of me now. You give everything in my life meaning.'

She drew her head away and they stared into each other's eyes, making up for all those days apart, before she sought out his ear. She whispered with a smile, 'These past few months have been so magical... I never realised it would feel so incredible to be so loved, so supported, so encouraged. You give me a strength, a sense of security that allows me to take on the world with no fear.'

His arm circled her waist and they sat with her brow resting against his collarbone, neither talking, just drawing strength and pleasure from being together again, breathing as one.

Eventually he pulled back from her, a wariness growing in his eyes. 'I've invited my parents to stay with us for Christmas, along with Christos and Sofia.'

Amazed by the news of the invitation, Grace leaned even further back. 'You have?'

Andreas suddenly seemed nervous. He swallowed hard before he spoke. 'You have shown me the importance of family. And I want us to be surrounded by family. Our children will need their grandparents. Now that Christos and I have agreed to jointly take over the family firm it's time to build bridges for the future.'

Grace opened and closed her mouth a number of times as she tried to process everything he'd said. The invitation was a big step forward in Andreas's rebuilding of his relationship with his father. 'I'm so glad.'

'You must invite Matt and Lizzie to join us too.'

She couldn't think of anything better. 'That's a wonderful idea. Thank you.'

'It's your home too, Grace, there's no need to thank me. In fact I think we should make it official that it belongs to you.'

He moved off the step and knelt down before her. Grace gave a little gasp. His eyes met hers, gently teasing her with tender affection. From his trouser pocket he took out a navy velvet pouch. And from the pouch a solitaire diamond ring. He held it out to her. The huge stone sparkled brightly under the winter sun.

'The past six months have been incredible, but I want the whole world to know how much I love you. I want to introduce you to others as my wife. I want us to start a family. Will you marry me?'

Was this really happening? Was the man she loved with every cell of her body asking her to spend the rest of her life with him? *Did dreams like this actually come true?*

'Are you sure? Even after living with me for six months and knowing now how talkative I am?'

'I'm sure.'

'Even knowing how easily I cry?'

'It just makes me want to hold you in my arms all the more.'

'What about my addiction to the Bee Gees?'

He gave a sigh. 'You might have a point...there's only so much *Saturday Night Fever* a man can take.'

'And then there's my obsession with cheese and marmalade sandwiches.'

'Now, *that* could be a problem—and you haven't even mentioned how you like to steal my clothes.'

'Only a sweater every now and again—and anyway you can't talk...you stole my nightdress.'

He held his hands up and gave a guilty grin. 'True.'

Oh, Lord, when he smiled like that life just felt incredible.

His hand rested on her knee. 'I love you, Grace. I know I can be bad-humoured at times, when I'm under pressure, and that I prefer silence to music, that I'm not the best at talking about my feelings, and I've no interest in television programmes like you... But I'd happily sit and listen to you giggle at some sitcom for the rest of my life. Before you I had no future other than work and the endless pursuit of success. Now I can see a life of happiness and fulfilment with you, and hopefully with our own family.' With a playful wince he added, 'Now, can you please answer me before my knees give way?'

Grace sat dazed. In the past six months Andreas had proved time and time again what a passionate, tender and strong man he was. He supported her unconditionally in her business plans, told her endlessly how beautiful and clever she was. Looked at her as though she was the only woman in the world.

'Andreas Petrakis, I fell in love with you the moment

you passed me your jacket the first night we met. I knew that behind that scowl lay a man with a good heart. I love you so much. Of *course* I'll be your wife.'

Eyes aglow with happiness, Andreas stood and pulled her up and into his arms. First he placed the ring on her finger, and then he tilted her face up to him.

'I promise to honour and treasure you for ever.'

His kiss was deep and passionate, their bodies pressed hard together.

When he eventually pulled away, he tucked her loose hair behind her ear and said, 'Close the shop early tonight. We have a whole week of being apart to make up for.'

Grace nodded but, unable to bear the thought of being without him, dragged him into the shop with her. He held her close from behind, his hands wrapped around her waist, his mouth nuzzling her neck while she shut down the till. Together they pulled down the shutters, and in the near darkness, surrounded by the sweet, heavenly scent of flowers, they smiled into each other's eyes.

A single soul inhabiting two bodies.

* * * * *

MILLS & BOON®
Hardback – August 2016

ROMANCE

The Di Sione Secret Baby	Maya Blake
Carides's Forgotten Wife	Maisey Yates
The Playboy's Ruthless Pursuit	Miranda Lee
His Mistress for a Week	Melanie Milburne
Crowned for the Prince's Heir	Sharon Kendrick
In the Sheikh's Service	Susan Stephens
Marrying Her Royal Enemy	Jennifer Hayward
Claiming His Wedding Night	Louise Fuller
An Unlikely Bride for the Billionaire	Michelle Douglas
Falling for the Secret Millionaire	Kate Hardy
The Forbidden Prince	Alison Roberts
The Best Man's Guarded Heart	Katrina Cudmore
Seduced by the Sheikh Surgeon	Carol Marinelli
Challenging the Doctor Sheikh	Amalie Berlin
The Doctor She Always Dreamed Of	Wendy S. Marcus
The Nurse's Newborn Gift	Wendy S. Marcus
Tempting Nashville's Celebrity Doc	Amy Ruttan
Dr White's Baby Wish	Sue MacKay
For Baby's Sake	Janice Maynard
An Heir for the Billionaire	Kat Cantrell

MILLS & BOON®
Large Print – August 2016

ROMANCE

The Sicilian's Stolen Son	Lynne Graham
Seduced into Her Boss's Service	Cathy Williams
The Billionaire's Defiant Acquisition	Sharon Kendrick
One Night to Wedding Vows	Kim Lawrence
Engaged to Her Ravensdale Enemy	Melanie Milburne
A Diamond Deal with the Greek	Maya Blake
Inherited by Ferranti	Kate Hewitt
The Billionaire's Baby Swap	Rebecca Winters
The Wedding Planner's Big Day	Cara Colter
Holiday with the Best Man	Kate Hardy
Tempted by Her Tycoon Boss	Jennie Adams

HISTORICAL

The Widow and the Sheikh	Marguerite Kaye
Return of the Runaway	Sarah Mallory
Saved by Scandal's Heir	Janice Preston
Forbidden Nights with the Viscount	Julia Justiss
Bound by One Scandalous Night	Diane Gaston

MEDICAL

His Shock Valentine's Proposal	Amy Ruttan
Craving Her Ex-Army Doc	Amy Ruttan
The Man She Could Never Forget	Meredith Webber
The Nurse Who Stole His Heart	Alison Roberts
Her Holiday Miracle	Joanna Neil
Discovering Dr Riley	Annie Claydon

MILLS & BOON®
Hardback – September 2016

ROMANCE

To Blackmail a Di Sione	Rachael Thomas
A Ring for Vincenzo's Heir	Jennie Lucas
Demetriou Demands His Child	Kate Hewitt
Trapped by Vialli's Vows	Chantelle Shaw
The Sheikh's Baby Scandal	Carol Marinelli
Defying the Billionaire's Command	Michelle Conder
The Secret Beneath the Veil	Dani Collins
The Mistress That Tamed De Santis	Natalie Anderson
Stepping into the Prince's World	Marion Lennox
Unveiling the Bridesmaid	Jessica Gilmore
The CEO's Surprise Family	Teresa Carpenter
The Billionaire from Her Past	Leah Ashton
A Daddy for Her Daughter	Tina Beckett
Reunited with His Runaway Bride	Robin Gianna
Rescued by Dr Rafe	Annie Claydon
Saved by the Single Dad	Annie Claydon
Sizzling Nights with Dr Off-Limits	Janice Lynn
Seven Nights with Her Ex	Louisa Heaton
The Boss's Baby Arrangement	Catherine Mann
Billionaire Boss, M.D.	Olivia Gates

MILLS & BOON®
Large Print – September 2016

ROMANCE

Morelli's Mistress	Anne Mather
A Tycoon to Be Reckoned With	Julia James
Billionaire Without a Past	Carol Marinelli
The Shock Cassano Baby	Andie Brock
The Most Scandalous Ravensdale	Melanie Milburne
The Sheikh's Last Mistress	Rachael Thomas
Claiming the Royal Innocent	Jennifer Hayward
The Billionaire Who Saw Her Beauty	Rebecca Winters
In the Boss's Castle	Jessica Gilmore
One Week with the French Tycoon	Christy McKellen
Rafael's Contract Bride	Nina Milne

HISTORICAL

In Bed with the Duke	Annie Burrows
More Than a Lover	Ann Lethbridge
Playing the Duke's Mistress	Eliza Redgold
The Blacksmith's Wife	Elisabeth Hobbes
That Despicable Rogue	Virginia Heath

MEDICAL

The Socialite's Secret	Carol Marinelli
London's Most Eligible Doctor	Annie O'Neil
Saving Maddie's Baby	Marion Lennox
A Sheikh to Capture Her Heart	Meredith Webber
Breaking All Their Rules	Sue MacKay
One Life-Changing Night	Louisa Heaton

MILLS & BOON®

Why shop at millsandboon.co.uk?

Each year, thousands of romance readers find their perfect read at millsandboon.co.uk. That's because we're passionate about bringing you the very best romantic fiction. Here are some of the advantages of shopping at www.millsandboon.co.uk:

* **Get new books first**—you'll be able to buy your favourite books one month before they hit the shops

* **Get exclusive discounts**—you'll also be able to buy our specially created monthly collections, with up to 50% off the RRP

* **Find your favourite authors**—latest news, interviews and new releases for all your favourite authors and series on our website, plus ideas for what to try next

* **Join in**—once you've bought your favourite books, don't forget to register with us to rate, review and join in the discussions

Visit **www.millsandboon.co.uk**
for all this and more today!